SOMETHING BORROWED IN SEABURY

SEABURY - BOOK 14

BETH RAIN

Copyright © 2025 by Beth Rain

Something Borrowed in Seabury (Seabury: Book 14)

First Publication: 14th February, 2025

All rights reserved.

No part of this book may be reproduced in any form or by any electronic or mechanical means, including information storage and retrieval systems. Except for use in any review, the reproduction or utilization of this work, in whole or in part, in any form by any electronic, mechanical or other means now known or hereafter invented, is forbidden without the written permission of the publisher.

Published by Beth Rain. The author may be contacted by email on bethrainauthor@gmail.com

❦ Created with Vellum

CHAPTER 1

MATT

Matt Pepper stepped off the bus at the far end of North Beach just as a yawn body-snatched him. Dumping his heavy backpack onto the pavement, he rested his hands on his knees and gave in to the wave of exhaustion that crashed over him. When he straightened up at last, he sucked in a deep breath, revelling in the salty tang of the fresh sea air.

'I'm home,' he whispered, staring around him. 'I can't believe it.'

What had it been... twelve years? No – more like fifteen!

Matt felt a bit like he was inside a dream.

He was really here - he was back in Seabury!

A strange tingle of joy mixed with something else snuck its way down his spine.

What was that? Anxiety? Fear? Grief?

Matt shook his head. He was far too tired to do any

soul-searching right now! He'd been travelling for far too long – and his body was putting up a protest. It was going to take a good long rest before he felt even halfway human again. He rolled his shoulders, wishing his tight muscles would give him a break from their near-constant ache.

'Fat chance of that,' he sighed, grabbing his bag and shuffling over towards the railings that separated the pavement from the pebbles of North Beach.

'What was I thinking?' he muttered, slumping against the railings and letting out another enormous yawn as he stared out to sea.

It had seemed like a great idea when he'd asked the bus driver to drop him off at North Beach. Sure, it was on the opposite side of town to Seabury House, but he'd thought a nice long walk would be the perfect way to get reacquainted with the little town.

That momentary lapse in judgement now meant he had quite a walk ahead of him... all the way through the centre of Seabury, up the hill towards the allotments, and then along the lanes that wound towards the secret valleys and coves where Seabury House stood. He had a feeling he'd be dragging his feet before he reached home!

'Home?' he sighed. He wasn't entirely sure he was allowed to use that word about Seabury House anymore. Technically, the place was one-quarter his— Matt's mum had gifted it to him and his three brothers when she'd moved abroad years ago—but he hadn't actually set foot inside the old building since he was a teenager.

There was that strange tingling again!

Turning his back on the sea, Matt rested against the railings and peered around, willing his brain to catch up.

'Doesn't look like much has changed!' he murmured, unable to keep a sleepy smile from spreading across his face as he eyeballed the windows of the Post Office across the road. It looked exactly the same as it had done when he was a kid – right down to the shelf of old-fashioned sweets he could just about make out behind the counter. He and his brothers had loved piling in there for a bag full of their favourites while Doris, the owner, gently reminded them all to brush their teeth before bed.

Matt glanced excitedly towards Nanna's Ice Cream Parlour then let out a sad groan. Clearly, some things *had* changed. The little shop was empty, the windows dark – with nothing to show other than a curling poster tacked to the glass.

Grabbing his bag, Matt pushed off the railings and headed over for a closer look. The sign was for a pop-up art exhibition that was long since over.

'Lionel Barclay?' he murmured.

The artist's name was a blast from the past. That was the stately gent who lived on the top floor of the Pebble Street Hotel… though how he put up with the awful owner, Veronica Hughes, was anyone's guess.

Shouldering his pack, Matt turned and set off in the direction of West Beach - though his determined stride slowed considerably as he stared with longing through the windows of a smart-looking new coffee shop.

'New York Froth?' he murmured. 'Nice!'

The temptation to nip in and grab himself a takeaway was almost overwhelming, but he really needed a shower—and maybe a nap too— before forcing the locals to have any kind of interaction with him!

'Morning! Coming in?'

Matt turned his head blearily, only to find a man holding the café door open for him.

Gah, how long had he been waiting?!

'Oh, no thanks!' said Matt, giving his head a little shake. 'Sorry, I'm away with the fairies.'

'Nothing a good coffee won't sort out,' urged the man.

Matt was fairly sure he'd never met the guy before... this was just the standard Seabury friendliness at work. He smiled and shook his head again, determined to resist temptation. 'I'm good, thanks... but I'll definitely be back once I've settled in a bit.'

'You're always welcome. Just tell them at the counter that Mike said your first coffee's on the house. Catch you soon!'

'Wow, thanks!' said Matt – but he was too late. Mike had already disappeared inside the café with a cheery wave.

Reluctantly, Matt forced himself to turn away from the rich, creamy aroma of good coffee. Picking up his pace, he cursed the straps of his pack as they started to rub. It had been all over the world with him and not caused an ounce of discomfort, but somehow—now that he was so close to home—the thing seemed to be fighting back.

'Morning!'

A grey-haired woman smiled at Matt as she bustled along the pavement towards him. The basket slung over the crook of her elbow made him do a double take. He knew that basket! This *had* to be Doris. So… she did still run the Post Office then?

'Good morning,' said Matt with a broad grin. He automatically slowed his pace, preparing himself for a thorough questioning by one of Seabury's matriarchs. Much to his surprise, all he got was a raised eyebrow and a brief nod before Doris hurried on by.

'Huh!' he muttered. She clearly hadn't recognised him.

He really had been gone for too long.

A spear of sadness pierced the tired fog hanging around him. It felt like someone had just stabbed him in the chest with a blunt spoon.

'Don't be an idiot!' he muttered, lengthening his stride again. He should be glad that Doris hadn't stopped to interrogate him – after all, he wasn't in any fit state to catch her up on the last fifteen years.

As he approached the Pebble Street Hotel, Matt

picked up his pace even further and kept his eyes on the pavement. If Veronica Hughes was hovering around the entrance, the last thing he wanted to do was make eye contact and be forced to speak to the old baggage! She was one person he had no interest in catching up with while he was in town.

Matt was just fighting a second bout of caffeine-scented temptation in the shape of the cutest little café called The Sardine, when a shout from behind him brought him to a halt.

'Matt Pepper? Matthew?'

Matt turned. 'Charlie?'

The bright eyes that met his hadn't changed a jot. Sure, there were a few more lines on the tanned face, and Charlie's favourite cap was looking more worn and sun-bleached than ever – but other than that, he was still the same old Charlie.

'What's on then, boy?' said Charlie, holding out his hand.

Matt shook his weathered paw and the deep sadness that had been threatening to settle evaporated under the old man's sunny smile. Even the greeting was comfortingly familiar. They were the exact words Charlie had uttered when he'd helped to fish both Matt and his bike out of a ditch near the allotments.

What's on then, boy?

And when he'd caught him scrumping apples.

What's on then, boy?

On that memorable occasion, instead of scolding

him, Charlie had handed him a bundle of fresh peapods to add to his bounty.

'It's so good to see you!' said Matt, as a flood of warmth threatened to clog his throat with happiness. Somehow, Charlie's greeting made him feel like it had only been a few days since they'd last seen each other. 'What's new?'

'How much time have you got, lad?' chuckled Charlie, falling into step beside him. 'I'm a married man now... though maybe someone's already told you about that?'

Matt shook his head. 'I hadn't heard, congratulations! Who's the lucky lady?'

'You remember Ethel?' said Charlie.

'Of course,' said Matt. 'No wonder you look so happy – it must be all that fresh cake!'

'Aye!' said Charlie with a grin. He patted his non-existent stomach. 'Thank heavens for all the digging I have to do up at the allotments, else I'd be the size of a house.'

'The allotments are still up there, then?' said Matt.

'Of course,' said Charlie. 'In fact, there are more of us up there now than ever. Tis thriving!'

'That's good,' said Matt. 'I can't imagine Seabury without them. Mind you, I thought the same thing about Nana's, and I see that's gone.'

Charlie nodded. 'Frank—the last owner—fell in love and moved to a small island off the top of Scotland.'

'That sounds like something Ewan would do!' laughed Matt.

'Speaking of Ewan, how are those brothers of yours?' said Charlie.

Matt shrugged. He didn't really have an answer to that. It wasn't just his old friends back in Seabury he'd lost contact with over the last few years.

'I've not heard much from them...' he hedged. He felt bad about being deliberately vague, but it wasn't the moment to start prodding the sore bit of his heart where his brothers had taken roost. He missed them... but he didn't have a clue how to solve that particular problem right now.

'So...' said Charlie, clearly hunting for a change of topic, 'I'm guessing you're back for Lionel's wedding, then?'

'Lionel's getting married too?' gasped Matt.

'Aye!' said Charlie. 'Didn't you know?'

Matt shook his head. 'Blimey, there must be something in the water around here!'

'You might be right about that,' said Charlie. 'Better watch yourself!'

'Ha! I barely have the energy to stay on my feet, let alone fall in love,' said Matt. Unable to stop himself, he let out a long sigh. 'I'm so out of the loop. I shouldn't have stayed away so long, but I've been out of the country a lot.'

'Aye, I heard,' said Charlie. 'Old Mrs Phillips told me

as much when I asked her if she knew where to send your wedding invitation.'

Matt nodded. He hadn't bothered letting the old housekeeper know where to find him. He never stayed still long enough for the information to be useful – and, if he was honest, he didn't really expect anyone from back home to try to reach him.

'Was it work that kept you away for so long?' said Charlie.

Matt nodded again. He didn't have the energy to go into it right now. As rewarding as his work had been, he knew he was teetering on the edge of burnout…

'Yep,' he said. 'Back for a bit of a break.'

Before he broke.

'Looks like you could do with it, too,' said Charlie, watching him closely as he swiped the back of his hand over his tired eyes.

'You're right about that!' said Matt as a yawn escaped him. 'Sorry… I think I'd better head up to the house before I fall asleep on my feet. With any luck, Mrs Phillips got my phone message and has unlocked the place!'

'Oh,' said Charlie. He raised his eyebrows, opened his mouth… then closed it again and shook his head.

'What?' said Matt, suddenly suspicious.

'Nothing at all,' said Charlie, not quite meeting his eye. 'I'm sure someone will have picked up your message.'

'If not, I'll just have to climb the wall,' said Matt, not

relishing the thought of having to battle his way through the thick, tangled ivy in order to reach his own front door.

'Now that really would be like old times!' chuckled Charlie.

CHAPTER 2

ROSIE

*R*osie Phillips threw the bedroom windows open and let out a sigh of relief as a wave of fresh air rushed into the room. Seabury House didn't smell *bad* exactly… just stuffy. But then, that was to be expected considering the poor old place had been left to its own devices for so long.

It was like all the love and joy that had once filled this sprawling family home had gone stale. It hadn't always been like this. She could remember when the house was full of the sound of boyish laughter, and Mr and Mrs Pepper's constant refrain of "Be careful boys!" and "Stop running!" and "DON'T do that to your brother!"

Rosie grinned at the memory. She'd regularly been the fifth tearaway – joining the four brothers to hurtle up and down the halls before being kicked out to run wild in the garden, surrounded and protected by its high, ivy-clad wall.

Her grandmother had been the Peppers' housekeeper as far back as she could remember, and Rosie had spent most of her childhood either at her little cottage just down the hill, or tagging along as she did her duties at Seabury House.

Rosie had naturally become an honorary sister to the four brothers... as well as best friends with the oldest boy – Matt.

'And then, more than best friends...' she sighed, leaning against the windowsill and staring out at the overgrown garden beyond.

For a couple of wonderful months when they were teenagers, Matt and Rosie had been inseparable. Ridiculously happy... and blissfully unaware of just how cruel life could be.

Mr Pepper's heart attack had changed everything. One day he'd been the jovial head of the family, and the next, he'd collapsed on the soft grass not far below this very window.

Rosie swallowed a lump of emotion, blinking hard as unshed tears turned the garden into a blur of watercolour. It was Matt who'd found his father. Matt who'd called for the ambulance that arrived far too late to help. Matt who'd turned into someone unreachable overnight.

The problem was, Rosie never had the chance to make things right—or even to grasp that such a thing simply wasn't possible. Before she knew what was happening, all four Pepper boys were shipped off to boarding school. Weeks later, Mrs Pepper moved to Spain and left Rosie's nan to keep an eye on the place until the boys were old enough to figure out what to do with it. Rosie hadn't seen any of them since.

Giving herself a shake, Rosie sniffed loudly as she rubbed her eyes on her sleeve. They'd been mere babies of fifteen and sixteen back then… now here she was, still cut up by the memory at the grand old age of thirty.

'Gah – I should never have agreed to do this job!' she muttered.

Of course, she knew that was a ridiculous thing to say. She'd never leave her nan in the lurch!

Even after decades of sweeping, tidying, cooking, and cleaning, Prudence Phillips still wasn't ready to hang up her apron strings. She loved her job. Of course, with the Pepper brothers scattered to the four winds, keeping an eye on the house was a lot easier than it had once been. Or at least… it *had* been easier until her nan had taken a nasty tumble and hurt her hip.

The idea of having to give up her job had been even more painful than the injury itself, so as well as moving back into the cottage to care for her nan while she recovered, Rosie had agreed to step in at Seabury House while she was at it.

Temporarily!

She kept reminding both herself and her nan of that fact. Not that it was hard work – far from it, in fact. It was just a bit strange to be surrounded by so many bittersweet memories.

Still, as jobs went, it was fairly easy-going. With no one in residence to run around after, Rosie's chief duties revolved around making sure the old electrics were behaving themselves, checking for leaks, and keeping an eye out for any signs of infestation – be it rodent or woodworm!

Other than that, Rosie just had to forward any mail to a PO Box based in London and do her best to keep on top of the dusting... not that she could see much point in that bit. Most of the furniture was covered with dust sheets, and there was no one around to worry about such things, anyway.

At least... that had been the case until today!

Rosie had returned to the cottage from her early morning run, only to find her nan in a flap. Someone had left a message on her answering machine. Someone male... with the surname Pepper.

Unfortunately, that was all the pair of them had managed to deduce about the caller, even after listening to the message a dozen or more times. Rosie might have been like a sister to the boys way back when, but these days she doubted she'd be able to identify them in a line-up—let alone tell their voices apart!

It didn't help that the line was terrible. It crackled

and popped and lost two words out of every three. Whoever was on the other end had clearly been in a hurry too.

Between them, Rosie and her nan had managed to piece together two key facts. One of the Pepper brothers was on his way home, and he would be in Seabury before dark. Which brother and how long he'd be staying for were both questions that were still very much up in the air!

'As long as it's not Matt!' Rosie muttered. 'Urgh!' she added with a shudder.

Who was she kidding? There had never been anything "urgh" about Matt Pepper!

He might have only been a lad the last time she'd set eyes on him, but Rosie had never forgotten how gorgeous he'd been. How kind and gentle... funny and warm.

'Didn't stop him from breaking your heart though, did it?' she grumbled to herself. Then she pulled a face. It wasn't his fault. He was just a kid whose entire life had been turned upside down in the blink of an eye. As for her? She'd simply been collateral damage.

Well... if it *was* Matt on his way home, she'd just have to face him like a grown-up! Right now, she needed to focus on getting the house ready to receive a guest for the first time in over a decade.

The morning's message had left her very little time to get the place presentable. After a frantic discussion with her nan, they'd decided the best thing would be to focus on getting the kitchen and all four of the brothers' bedrooms aired and cleaned. At least that way, they'd be ready for whoever turned up!

It had been a mad, mad morning. Rosie had hoovered and dusted for all she was worth. She'd stripped all four of the brothers' beds and – not daring to trust the ancient washing machine and tumble dryer at Seabury House – she'd shlepped back to the cottage to do the laundry.

At long last, she was nearly finished. There was just this last bed to make, and then she'd be able to nip into town to shop for a few basics. Rosie had brought a small bottle of milk and some tea bags with her from her nan's, but she wanted to replace the decades-old soap in the bathrooms and stock the fridge with something that could be cobbled together for breakfast.

'Right, let's do this,' sighed Rosie, rolling her shoulders. She'd put this room off for as long as she could. It was full of glimpses into a boyish childhood – from the glow-in-the-dark stars stuck to the ceiling to the posters on the walls. It was also full of memories – hours spent listening to music and whispered plans for a future that had never happened.

Matt's room.

Rosie shook her head and strode over to the bed. Grabbing the dinosaur duvet cover from the linen basket, she gave it a good shake. If it *was* Matt on his way home, she wondered what he'd make of having to sleep under his ancient childhood duvet again. A small smile fought its way onto her face at the thought.

The other rooms had been the same – firmly caught in a time warp. They were full of posters and toys, trains and smudges where inky fingers had trailed against the once-expensive wallpaper. Rosie might have opened the windows and washed everything down, but there was no wiping away the traces of the past.

With one last flick of her wrist, Rosie tossed the newly covered pillow into place and smoothed her palm over the cover to banish the creases.

'There, that's much better,' she said. She quickly folded the old, multicoloured crochet blanket and added it to the foot of the bed before glancing around the rest room to check she hadn't missed anything obvious.

The cobwebs were gone, and the layer of dust had disappeared.

'Window!' she muttered.

The last thing she needed was for one of the dozens of blackbirds – who'd claimed the abandoned, overgrown garden as their private playground – to slip inside and make a mess! Grabbing the latch, she yanked at it until there was just a narrow gap left – enough to let the fresh air in minus any unwanted visitors.

Rosie frowned out at the tangled garden again. If only she had time to do something about the mess out there too. It wasn't exactly in her job description, but it seemed a shame that Mrs Pepper's beautiful flower beds had become choked with weeds and the paths laced with bramble tripwires.

Here and there, hints of pink and yellow peeped out from beneath the mess – remnants of years gone by, still doing their best to bloom. It could be gorgeous out there again if only someone took the time to rediscover it.

'Not today,' she muttered. She had enough to be getting on with!

Rosie was just about to turn away when a movement caught her eye. It was probably just another blackbird, but...

She froze and watched as the old wooden gate set deep into the ivy-covered wall creaked open.

'What on earth?'

No one other than Rosie, her nan, and the occasional lost tourist used that gate! It opened onto the narrow footpath that led towards her nan's cottage, and then eventually back into town. Rosie always locked it behind her when she left for the day, but there didn't seem much point when she was in the house.

'Seriously, I don't have time for this!' she huffed, watching as a bewildered-looking man with a huge backpack edged into the garden. He stopped and stared around.

Clearly, Rosie had a curious tourist on her hands. Her nan had warned her about this. They turned up occasionally, wanting to explore the walled garden.

Not on her watch!

Rosie trotted out of the room and took the stairs two at a time. She'd get rid of the walker and then head down to town. Then, when she'd stocked the fridge and given the kitchen one last go-over, she'd leave the main driveway gates open so that whichever Pepper brother turned up, they'd be able to drive right up to the house.

'Excuse me,' yelled Rosie, throwing the front door open and marching outside. 'Excuse me, this is private property.'

The tall stranger turned to face her, and Rosie gasped.

Oh no, oh no!

She came to a screeching halt, sending a spray of weedy gravel flying in the process. Breathing hard, she stared at the man who'd changed so much... and not at all.

There were four of them - why did it have to be him?!

Matt Pepper stared right back at her, looking tall, tanned and... tired.

'Rosie?' Matt blinked in confusion. He looked a bit like he'd seen a ghost... and Rosie knew exactly how he felt. 'What on earth are you doing here?'

'You called and left a message,' she said, sounding a bit pouty even to her own ears. 'I'm the new housekeeper. Well... the temporary one.'

'You are?' said Matt, surprise written all over his face.

Rosie nodded, wondering what she should do next.

What were you meant to do when you came face to face with the boy who broke your heart when you were a kid, even though it really wasn't his fault?!

Should she hug him? Shake his hand?

'Why don't you come on in?' she said. Then she cringed, realising that she'd just invited him into his own house.

'That's the plan,' said Matt, looking bemused.

'Good. Okay... good.'

Rosie turned her back to him and rolled her eyes at herself so hard they felt like they might pop out. She'd had almost fifteen years to plan what to say if she ever saw him again. Was that *really* the best she could come up with?!

CHAPTER 3

MATT

Matt willed his thumping heart to behave itself. He was sweating profusely, and by the feel of things, he was probably bright pink in the face too. As much as he'd love to blame it all on the long walk from the other side of town, he knew he'd just be kidding himself.

This was all down to Rosie Phillips!

He hadn't set eyes on her in… well… in what felt like forever. It had been another lifetime. A decidedly happier lifetime—or at least, it had been before it all fell apart.

Rosie was the last person Matt expected to find waiting for him at Seabury House… and the last person he wanted to witness him in his current state of pure discombobulation. If it had occurred to him that she'd be his welcoming party, he'd have done his best to smarten up a bit. As it was, Matt was pretty sure he looked like something that had been dragged through a hedge backwards. Repeatedly.

The last thing Matt heard, Rosie was living somewhere near Exeter. Even so, he'd known there was a slight chance he might bump into her while he was back in town. After all, her grandmother *was* their housekeeper. He'd just thought he'd have a bit more time to prepare himself for this ultimate blast from the past.

Not that it meant anything to him, of course.

He never thought about Rosie.

Much.

Not more than once or twice a day, at least!

The problem was, thinking about Rosie tended to lead to memories of his dad... of finding him prone on the grass in this very garden. Then everything would tie itself up in a vast, grief-filled tangle he never quite managed to sort out.

This was why he'd kept himself busy. It was also why he hadn't set foot in Seabury for so long!

Matt stared after Rosie. She was heading back towards the house, her perky ponytail swinging from side to side. She'd been seriously cute when she was younger. Now, though, Rosie Phillips wasn't just cute—she was beautiful. Jaw-dropping, spear-through-the-heart kind of beautiful.

Shifting from one foot to the other, Matt winced as his pack pinched his sore skin. He needed to put it down. He needed the loo. He needed a nap in a blissfully darkened room... but first, he needed to get rid of Rosie without coming across as completely rude!

It wasn't that he wasn't glad to see her... it was all just a bit... much.

Matt sighed. He was so tired he could barely string a coherent thought together, let alone a sentence. With a little shake of his head, he dragged one leaden foot after the other and did his best to catch up.

'Hang on a sec,' he puffed, 'if you're the new housekeeper, where's your nan?'

The minute the words left his mouth, Matt could have kicked himself. What if Mrs Phillips had passed away?! After all, she'd seemed ancient back when they were kids! Plus, she hadn't answered her phone when he'd called that morning.

Rosie paused and turned towards him with one eyebrow raised. He couldn't tell if she was sad... angry... upset...

'Sorry, I...' he trailed off. He wasn't sure what he was sorry about. He wasn't sure about anything right now other than the fact that he really wanted to go to sleep. 'Sorry,' he said again.

'It's fine,' said Rosie, with an eye roll that was so familiar it almost brought tears to his eyes. 'Nan had a fall. She's on the mend now, but I'm back at the cottage with her until she's fully back on her feet.'

'And you took over here too?' said Matt, glad he hadn't managed to put his foot in it in the worst way possible.

'Temporarily,' said Rosie. 'Sorry it's such a surprise. We had no idea any of you were planning to come back. Anyway, I'm pretty sure Nan tried to let one of you know what was happening!'

'I'm sure she did,' said Matt hurriedly. He didn't want to get into the fact that he hadn't spoken to his brothers in ages. 'I only arrived back in the country yesterday.'

'Oh,' said Rosie, cocking her head. 'Well, that explains it.'

'Explains what?' said Matt.

'The fact that you gave us such short notice about turning up!' she said, turning her back on him and striding towards the front door again.

Matt followed her, doing his best not to get hypnotised by her swinging ponytail.

It had been a last-minute phone call because it had been a last-minute decision to come home to Seabury. He needed a rest and some peace and quiet. Staggering through the airport in search of his pack the previous evening, Seabury House had seemed like the best solution.

Now, though, he wasn't so sure!

Peace and quiet? Fat chance of that with Rosie Phillips around!

A small smile crept onto Matt's face. The girl he remembered had the habit of going into auto-witter mode at the drop of a hat. It didn't matter how she was feeling – excited, nervous, worried, tired, happy, sad…

even hungry... Rosie could talk the hind legs off a donkey.

She wasn't exactly chatty right now, though, was she?!

Clearly, the one emotion that had the power to stop her in her tracks was shock. No doubt that would wear off before too long, though! Sure, it had been a seriously long time since Matt had last seen her – and they'd hardly parted on the best of terms – but somehow, he couldn't imagine Rosie Phillips had come over all quiet and mysterious!

Then again, maybe she had. A lot could change in fifteen years. Just because his life had been caught in some kind of weird, suspended animation, it didn't mean the rest of the world had come to a grinding halt too.

For all he knew, Rosie had a partner. Hell, she was probably married... she might even be a mother...

The thought walloped Matt in the chest at the exact moment he stepped through the doorway into Seabury House. The scent of dust and lavender polish slammed into him, and he blinked, swaying on the spot as the past rushed to greet him.

'Are you okay?' said Rosie. She'd turned to face him and was eyeballing him with concern.

'Huh?' said Matt.

'Would you like some tea... or a sandwich or...' Rosie trailed off.

'I think I'll just settle in,' said Matt, shaking his head.

'Are you sure?' she said, not taking her eyes off him.

'You've gone all pale. When was the last time you had something to eat?'

Matt shrugged. He wasn't quite sure. It didn't matter, anyway. All he wanted right now was to go to sleep. Food was beyond him. A rest and a bit of time alone in his old home would help him get his bearings again. Then he'd think about food... and what he wanted to do about the rest of it... the rest of his life.

'Matt?' said Rosie, this time her voice was gentle and laced with concern.

'I'm good. Jetlag, that's all,' he invented. 'I'll eat after a nap. I think I need to head upstairs.'

He took a couple of purposeful steps towards the broad staircase, hoping she might take the hint and let him disappear up to his bedroom alone.

Fat chance of that!

Rosie leapt into action and scuttled forwards, trotting up the stairs before Matt had even reached them. He paused briefly and then shrugged again. He didn't have the energy to argue.

Taking the stairs slowly, Matt gripped the banister for support as the scent of lavender and the feel of the smooth wood under his palm threatened to sweep him away again. Everything was so achingly familiar... and yet somehow so different to his closely guarded memories of the old house.

He was halfway up the stairs when he realised what was different. His childhood had been full of chaos and noise. There had never been a moment's peace with four boys under the same roof. Now, though, the air hung heavy with more than a decade's worth of silence.

'I've done my best to get the place ready for you,' said Rosie as she waited for him at the top of the stairs. 'I wasn't sure which one of you was coming home though…'

'But the message…?' said Matt. It was as much as he could manage. The stairs were sapping him of his last ounce of energy.

'It was really garbled,' said Rosie. 'I think you were out of signal or something. Nan and I listened to it loads of times, but we couldn't figure it out. All we could tell was that one of you would be back today, sometime before dark.'

Matt nodded. At least that explained why Rosie had looked like she'd seen a ghost when she spotted him in the garden!

'Anyway,' said Rosie, budging over slightly so that he could join her on the gloomy landing, 'I aired and cleaned all four of your bedrooms – and I've washed the bedding and made the beds. Of course, if you don't want to stay in your childhood bedroom, I can always get one of the others ready for tomorrow…?'

Matt shook his head. 'It's fine. Great. Thank you.'

He didn't really care either way. The mention of the word 'bedroom' had felt like a clunk over the head with a big, fluffy mallet.

'The kitchen's clean and ready to go too,' said Rosie, leading the way along the hall. 'I just need to pop into town for some basics for you – though there's milk and some teabags down there if you get desperate.'

Matt blinked and did his best to keep up as Rosie started to list things she was planning to shop for. Auto-witter mode was clearly back in full force! He turned into his childhood bedroom, hoping that it might stop her in her tracks, but she simply followed him.

'Oh, it's much better in here,' she said, crossing the room and closing the window. 'I wanted to let some fresh air in here. Don't want you to get cold, though!'

'Cheers,' said Matt, wincing as he struggled with the straps of his pack. Dumping it on the floor, he let out a sigh of relief. 'Right, I'm just going to fall into bed for a bit. It's been a long few days.'

'Oh. Right. Of course!' said Rosie.

Matt waited for her to leave, but she didn't budge.

He cleared his throat. What did he have to do to make her clear off? The bed was beckoning, and he had a feeling if he looked hard enough, the dinosaur on the duvet cover was probably calling his name!

'So… if there's anything you need, just give me a shout,' said Rosie.

Matt nodded, only just resisting the urge to start herding her towards the door.

'Ah – you don't have my mobile number though, do you?' she said. 'Do you have your phone?'

Matt shook his head. It was in his pack somewhere. Its battery was as flat as a pancake, and there was no way he was going on the hunt for the charger right now.

'Oh,' said Rosie with a frown. 'Well... how about...'

Matt bit his tongue and held in a little growl of frustration as she turned and strode over to the desk in the corner. He watched, swaying slightly, as she grabbed an ancient exercise book and a crayon and scrawled something on the back page.

'There. If you think of anything, you can let me know!' she said brightly.

Matt nodded, doing his best to smile at her... though he had a feeling it was probably more of a grimace.

'Have a good rest,' she said, moving towards the door.

Finally!

Matt followed her, hoping to block any chance of her making another unscheduled dive back into the bedroom. The minute she stepped into the hall, he gently but firmly closed the door in her face. Then he turned towards the bed and collapsed—face-first—onto the dinosaur duvet.

CHAPTER 4

ROSIE

'You're such an idiot!' Rosie hissed.

She'd been muttering this on a non-stop loop for at least an hour. It had provided a cringe-making soundtrack that had taken her all the way down to town for some shopping, then all the way back up the hill and along the lanes. Now, it was echoing around the kitchen of Seabury House as she filled the fridge and cupboards with enough goodies to keep Matt going for a couple of days.

Matt. ARGH!

Rosie shook her head as yet another wave of pure mortification swept over her. She'd hoped the brisk walk into town might burn off some of the embarrassment. Instead, it had simply fuelled it.

The sight of Matt Pepper striding into his childhood home had done something strange to her brain. After the initial shock of seeing him had worn off, she'd promptly developed the worst case of verbal diarrhoea she'd ever encountered. She hadn't even been able to stop herself from talking when she'd followed him into his bedroom.

'Gah!' she groaned.

The poor guy might have been dead on his feet, but he'd still had to usher her out of his bedroom so that he could take a nap.

Rosie felt a hot blush stain her cheeks yet again.

'Stupid idiot,' she muttered. 'Stupid, stupid idiot!'

She needed to get out of Seabury House and hot-foot it back to her Nan's cottage to lick her wounds.

But... what if Matt needed her?

Why a grown man in his own home would suddenly need her was anyone's guess. After all, Matt Pepper had survived perfectly well without her since he was sixteen years old. Even so, something about him was worrying Rosie. Sure, he was tanned, tall, lean and handsome... but there was something else lurking beneath the surface. Something she couldn't quite put her finger on.

There were dark circles underneath Matt's eyes that she couldn't imagine were entirely down to a bit of short-term jetlag. He was pale beneath his tan, too. It wasn't just that, though...

'Get a grip – you're losing the plot!' tutted Rosie, shaking her head.

Even so... she couldn't shake the idea that there was

something seriously *up* with the handsome Pepper boy she'd never quite managed to forget.

Straightening her shoulders, Rosie decided it was time to behave like the adult she supposedly was. If she didn't check on Matt before she left, she was going to drive herself barmy before bedtime. She'd just nip upstairs and triple-check he didn't need anything… and then she'd head back to her Nan's.

'Good plan!' she muttered, giving herself a mental pat on the back as she dashed out of the kitchen.

Halfway up the stairs, Rosie changed her mind. It wasn't because she'd chickened out… it was simply that the deep, rumbling snores coming from the direction of Matt's bedroom answered all her questions.

Yes, he was still alive up there.

No, he didn't want a cup of tea.

No, he didn't need anyone to spout nonsense at him while he was trying to take a nap.

Yes, she really should go home before she made an even bigger prat out of herself!

'You're back at last!'

The minute Rosie opened the front door to the cottage, her Nan's grinning face appeared in the hallway.

'What on earth are you doing on your feet!' gasped Rosie, hurrying to offer her Nan a steadying arm.

'Don't fuss!' chuckled Prudence, flapping her hands good-naturedly. 'It's good for me to be up and about. Anyway, it's just as well I am – you've been gone so long, I was about to send out a search party.'

'Sorry Nan… you should have called!' said Rosie, following her slow shuffle through to the cosy kitchen.

'I'm pulling your leg, love,' said Prudence, making her way over to the counter and flicking the kettle on. 'Now then… tell me everything. Which one came home?!'

Rosie grinned. She wasn't falling for any of this nonsense about needing to stretch her legs… she knew her Nan had probably been on the lookout for her return all afternoon, waiting for all the gossip she could get.

Shrugging off the last vestiges of embarrassment, Rosie prepared herself for a proper grilling.

'It's Matt,' she said, doing her best to keep her voice even.

'Oh dear, oh dear!' chuckled Prudence, turning to her with bright eyes. 'Well, that must have been interesting!'

'You could say that,' said Rosie, sinking down into one of the chairs at the kitchen table. She knew there was no point trying to help her Nan with the tea things – she'd only get shooed off. 'At first, I thought he was one of those annoying visitors who want to look around the garden, so I went outside to try to get rid of him!'

Prudence let out a chuckle of pure glee.

'Try not to enjoy my horror too much, Nan!' laughed Rosie.

'Ah, get away with you, girl,' said Prudence, rolling her eyes. 'Anyway, out with it. What's he like?'

'He's… gorgeous,' sighed Rosie. 'I mean, he always was, but it's like he's grown into his face or something.'

'Well, that's very nice, love,' said her Nan, still looking amused, 'but I wasn't really talking about his looks. What's he doing back in Seabury? What's he been up to? What's his life like now?'

Rosie took a sheepish sip of the tea her Nan had just poured for her in an attempt to put off the inevitable… but it didn't help. Prudence was still waiting for an answer when she put the cup down.

'You know,' she hedged, 'I didn't really get the chance to talk to him much.'

'Now, why do I find that hard to believe?' said Prudence. 'If you found him outside and then took him in, I can't imagine that's true. I know what you're like, Rosie Phillips! Probably more of a case that the poor boy couldn't get a word in edgeways?'

Rosie grinned. Her Nan knew first-hand what a chatterbox she was—especially when she was nervous. In fact, it was a trait she'd inherited from Prudence herself.

'Okay, fine, you're right – I probably didn't give the poor guy much airtime,' said Rosie. 'But in my defence, I don't think Matt was feeling particularly chatty anyway. He looked like he was dead on his feet, and I don't think it was all down to the *ghost of girlfriend past* materialising in front of him the minute he arrived home.'

'Dead on his feet?' said Prudence, looking concerned. 'Do you think he's ill?'

Rosie thought about it for a minute. 'Not sure,' she said. 'I mean... he looked pretty fit and tanned, but he looked knackered too. Pale. Dark circles under his eyes. All he wanted to do was go straight upstairs to bed. He didn't even want a cuppa!'

'Well,' said her Nan, sucking in a breath, 'that's never a good sign. I don't like the idea of him being in that big house all on his own. What if he needs a doctor?'

'I left him my mobile number, just in case,' said Rosie. 'I wanted to check in on him when I got back from doing a bit of shopping, but from the snoring coming from his bedroom, I don't think he's going to be waking up any time soon!'

'Well,' said Prudence, taking a delicate sip of tea, 'we'll just have to keep an eye on him and feed him up a bit while he's here.'

'I'm not sure that's in your job description anymore, Nan,' said Rosie with a grin. Prudence had spent a great deal of time making snacks for the four brothers when they were little—providing the grubby ragamuffins with sandwiches, cake and squash whenever they trouped into the kitchen covered in mud and scratches from whatever grand adventure they'd been having in the gardens of Seabury House.

'I don't care if it is or if it isn't,' said Prudence. 'You'll do it for me, won't you?'

'Me?' laughed Rosie. 'What… be on hand for regular bacon sarnie duty?'

Her Nan shook her head. 'Just make sure the boy's looking after himself. I don't like what you said about him looking all pale. He won't have a clue how much time you normally spend at the house, so he won't think it's strange if you're up there a bit more than usual.'

'You want me to spy on my ex-boyfriend?' said Rosie.

'No,' said Prudence, fixing her with a steady stare. 'I want you to make sure that a dear old friend is doing okay. And if he's not, I want you to do everything you can to help.'

Rosie swallowed. There it was… her ready-made excuse to spend extra time at Seabury House.

Extra time with Matt.

'Fine,' said Rosie. 'I will – but only because you asked me to.'

'Sure,' said her Nan, raising a mischievous eyebrow. 'Just for me. You keep telling yourself that, Rosie!'

'I'm not sure he'll want me hanging around though, Nan,' she said. 'I mean… he did dump me, remember.'

'Ah, you were both young,' said Prudence, waving her hand dismissively.

'He broke my heart,' said Rosie, the words coming out before she had the chance to stop them.

'I know, love,' said Prudence, her voice going soft. 'But only because losing his dad broke *his* heart. Matt didn't know whether he was coming or going. I'm still convinced the pair of you would have got back together if Mrs Pepper hadn't sent them all off to school like that.'

Rosie shrugged. She'd often wondered what would have happened if Matt hadn't disappeared from her life so suddenly. She'd wanted to reach out to him so many times over the years... but *he'd* never contacted *her*... and what would she have said anyway?

'So... you really didn't manage to get *any* gossip out of him before he fell asleep?'

Her Nan's voice dragged Rosie back to reality, and she shook her head, irritated with herself.

Get a grip! You're acting like a lovesick teenager!

'No, afraid not,' said Rosie.

'Well then – that's your other job while you're up at Seabury House,' said Prudence. 'I want to know what that boy's been up to all these years!'

'Why?' said Rosie.

'Because I'm a very old lady who's bored with being stuck in the house,' laughed Prudence. 'And because I loved those boys. It's not just *your* life they disappeared from.'

A pang of guilt hit Rosie in the chest. She glanced at

her Nan, wanting to apologise, only to find her sipping her tea with a decided twinkle in her eye.

'What?' said Rosie, instantly suspicious.

'Oh, nothing,' said Prudence. 'It's just nice to see you all worked up over something, Rosie Posy, that's all.'

'I'm not worked up!' huffed Rosie. 'I'm just exhausted from cleaning four bedrooms and that massive kitchen.'

'Exhausted, my Aunt Fanny!' her Nan chuckled.

'*Not* that it'll get used,' said Rosie, ignoring her Nan's gentle jab. 'Somehow, I can't imagine Matt cooking up a storm… can you?'

'Oh, you never know,' said Prudence. 'He might have been up to anything over the years. For all we know, he could be a fancy chef by now!'

'I just can't imagine it!' said Rosie.

'You've still got a soft spot for that boy,' said her Nan. 'That's one thing I *do* know.'

'I do *not* have a soft spot for him,' said Rosie, lying through her teeth. Matt Pepper would always be her first love—the one that got away because of the most heartbreaking circumstances. 'I just wish it was one of the others who'd decided to come home. It would have been a lot simpler.'

'Simpler?' said her Nan. 'Maybe. But not half as much fun.'

CHAPTER 5

MATT

Matt could vaguely hear the sound of bells in the distance, but he couldn't bring himself to open his eyes. He'd been having a wonderful dream… one where he'd finally drummed up the courage to head home to Seabury.

Bloody bells!

Scrunching his eyes closed even more tightly, Matt snuggled further beneath the covers. Maybe if he ignored the sound, it'd clear off. Then he could get back to his nap.

It didn't work. Even with his head firmly buried underneath several cosy layers, the incessant ringing continued to plague him.

He still couldn't quite place the sound. It was familiar… but it wasn't the *bing bong* of an airport alert telling customers it was time to board, nor the sound of his mobile phone telling him he had an appointment to get to.

Where on earth was he?

Rolling over, Matt cracked one eye open and pulled an ancient dinosaur duvet up to his chin. A colourful crochet blanket came with it, tickling his nose.

Of course – he was back in his childhood home!

So... it hadn't been a dream, then?

But what was with the bells?

Matt struggled to sit up and blinked as the strange but familiar shapes of his childhood bedroom came into focus.

Of course! The bells were another blast from the past!

A long-buried memory bubbled up to the surface—hurtling along the hall as he did his best to beat his three annoying little brothers to the ancient rotary phone.

'We've still got a landline?!' he muttered, letting out a huge yawn. He'd assumed it had been disconnected years ago. Then again, if he was being honest, he'd never given it so much as a passing thought. Matt had left the care of the house firmly in Mrs Phillips's capable hands, and he guessed his brothers had probably done exactly the same thing.

With a sigh, Matt rolled out of bed and promptly caught his foot in the crochet blanket. Giving his leg an impatient shake to free himself, he headed for the door. He was about to hurtle downstairs to answer the phone before it stopped ringing when he realised he wasn't wearing anything.

'Damn it!' he muttered.

It probably wasn't the best idea to streak downstairs—no matter how private Seabury House was with its high wall. Matt had no idea how long he'd been asleep, but knowing his luck, Rosie would be back from her shopping trip by now. It *really* wouldn't be polite to give her an eyeful!

Matt stood frozen in his nakedness for a couple more rings.

Surely, if Rosie was downstairs, she'd answer the phone?

Well, if he didn't do something soon, whoever was on the other end was going to give up.

Making a desperate grab for the crochet blanket, Matt snatched it from the floor and hastily wrapped it around his waist. It wasn't exactly big enough, and the wool was a fairly loose weave… but it was better than nothing!

Dashing for the door, Matt legged it down the stairs, hoping the old phone was still tucked away in the same shadowy recess where it had always been.

Skidding to a halt, he breathed a sigh of relief. He was in luck.

Matt grabbed the old-fashioned handset, doing his best to catch his breath.

'Hello?' he puffed.

'Matthew? Matt?'

Matt didn't have the chance to register much about

whoever was on the other end of the line because, at that moment, the front door crashed open, and Rosie stepped inside.

Matt's fingers tightened around the handful of blanket slung around his hips. Unfortunately, it didn't do anything to stop Rosie's eyes from going wide as they dropped to his waist... and beyond.

'Uh oh!' he muttered.

'Oh my GOODNESS!' squeaked Rosie, practically cricking her neck as she tore her eyes away from him to look directly up at the ceiling... then down to the floor. Next, she executed a lopsided sort of pirouette as she searched for an escape route.

'I'm *so* sorry!' muttered Matt as a wave of heat engulfed him. He had a nasty feeling he'd just managed to give the girl of his dreams a full-frontal view of meat and both vegetables.

GAH!

'Hello? Hello, Matt?' came a tinny voice in his ear. 'Hello? Is this line still working?'

Matt couldn't do anything other than grunt a response as he shuffled on the spot, angling the offending view towards the wall, only to realise that by doing so, he'd just treated Rosie to a *full moon* through the gap in the back of the blanket.

Rosie turned from red to purple. 'Erm... morning!' she squeaked, sidling past him and trotting in the direction of the kitchen.

'Whyyyyyy,' breathed Matt.

'Hello? Hello? Is everything all right?'

Matt gave his head a shake. Miraculously, there was still someone on the other end of the line. Thank heavens this wasn't a video call!

'Hi, sorry. Um, Bad line. Sorry,' he mumbled.

It wasn't a bad line. It was as clear as a bell, but there was no way he was about to admit the real reason he'd taken so long to answer.

'Matt, it's Charlie,' came the concerned voice again. 'Are you sure you're alright?'

Matt blinked. Charlie. Of course! He'd bumped into him on his walk home. No one apart from Charlie knew he'd be here… other than Rosie, of course…

'Everything's fine, Charlie,' said Matt, shaking his head and doing his best to dislodge the image of Rosie's wide eyes from his mind. He couldn't think about her right now! 'I just… erm… bumped into Rosie on my way downstairs, that's all.'

'Ah, I see,' said Charlie.

Matt cringed. Why did he get the feeling Charlie had some kind of x-ray vision?!

'Anyway,' said Charlie. 'I was wondering if you might have a moment to drop by the Pebble Street Hotel?'

'The hotel?' said Matt in surprise. He wasn't sure what he'd been expecting Charlie to say, but it definitely wasn't that.

'Yes,' said Charlie. 'Look, I guess I'd better own up. I'm afraid I rather let the cat out of the bag. I mentioned to Lionel that you're back in town. He's my best friend, see... and... well, I promise it was for a good reason.'

Matt opened his mouth to say something, but Charlie ploughed on.

'Full disclosure—I told Ethel too. Being the wife, I tell her everything.' He paused and then let out a little laugh. 'For the record, that's the key to a peaceful life!'

Matt grinned. 'I'll remember that. Anyway, don't worry about it. I'll have to come into town for supplies at some point, so I doubt my arrival would have stayed quiet for much longer!'

'Well, that's a relief,' said Charlie. 'So, you'll come by the hotel? Lionel wants to have a chat with you about something.'

'Lionel?' said Matt in surprise. He couldn't imagine what the old gent might want to talk to him about. They'd never really known each other beyond a respectful nod on his part and a cheery wave on Lionel's. 'Well... I don't see why not. I'm sure we can organise something before I leave town.'

'Hmm...' said Charlie. 'See, it's like this. It's a bit urgent. He really needs your help. Any chance you'd be willing to pop down in... say... the next couple of hours?'

Matt raised his eyebrows. Just because he hadn't kept in touch with his old friends from Seabury, it didn't mean they hadn't been keeping tabs on him. He had hoped that returning to town might mean he could leave his professional life behind - for a few weeks at least.

But... urgent was urgent. He couldn't say no.

'Of course,' said Matt, wishing he'd brought the basics home with him. 'I'll be down as soon as I can.'

Even as he said the words, his mind flew to Rosie. He had an apology to deliver to the kitchen before he went anywhere!

'Erm... will Lionel be okay if I'm an hour... maybe two? I have a couple of things to sort out, and then I'll need to walk into town.'

'Of course,' said Charlie. 'There's no rush. I'm with him now, so I'll let him know.'

'Sure?' said Matt.

'Positive lad, don't you worry.'

Matt replaced the handset and let out a sigh. It was all well and good for Charlie to tell him not to worry... but *he* wasn't the one who had to apologise for flashing the housekeeper! He could hear Rosie banging around in the kitchen... and... was that fresh toast he could smell?

Matt took a couple of steps towards the kitchen door and then thought better of it. Clothes first... grovelling apologies second!

CHAPTER 6

ROSIE

The kitchen door creaked, making Rosie jump. Cursing herself, she spun around with the butter knife still firmly in hand.

It was Matt. Of *course* it was Matt. She knew he'd reappear at some point. How could he not after that little *encounter* in the hallway?

'Hey!' she said, cringing as her voice came out in a high-pitched squeak. What did it say about her that she was more than a little bit disappointed that he was now fully dressed instead of wearing that decidedly revealing blanket?!

'Hi,' said Matt, sidling into the room and running a hand nervously through his hair.

His fingers left it standing up in damp little spikes, and Rosie couldn't help but smile. He might be in his early thirties, but this older, more knackered version of

Matt Pepper still reminded her of the young lad she'd once known.

'I… erm… I like your tee shirt!' she said, mainly to explain why she was staring—unblinking—at his broad chest. Just five minutes ago, she'd seen it in all its muscley glory.

She'd seen some of his other glory too, but that had been a bit further south!

'Oh, thanks!' said Matt, peering down at himself.

The tee shirt in question was clearly old and much-washed, with the words "I Love Hippos" emblazoned across the chest.

'So… hippos, huh?' she said.

'It was a stag-do thing,' he said, shifting from foot to foot, looking embarrassed.

'Oh!' Rosie felt her heart crash land on the kitchen tiles.

He was married? Of course he was married! Just because her life seemed to be on perpetual hold, it didn't mean everyone else was such a loser, did it?

'Well, congratulations… though I guess it's probably a bit late for that,' she said, turning her back on him and staring at the rapidly cooling slice of toast on the counter. For some reason, she'd lost her appetite.

Rosie swallowed. She needed to pull herself together… there was no way she wanted Matt to spot the mad swirl of emotions that were probably visible on her face right now.

'Late for what?' said Matt, sounding confused. 'Oh!

It wasn't *my* stag do. Thank God... the poor groom ended up in the middle of Poole Harbour in a dingy, wearing a grass skirt and pair of coconuts!'

Rosie let out a honk that was somewhere between a laugh and a hiccup. 'Coconuts?' she added lamely, turning to look at him again.

'Yep. A fine pair,' said Matt with a broad grin.

'So... *are* you married?' said Rosie. Then she shook her head. 'Sorry, that's personal and none of my business.'

'I'm not,' said Matt. 'Are you?'

'Nope,' she said.

'Engaged... in love... shacked up?' said Matt, wiggling his eyebrows.

'That'd be nope, uh-uh, and not anymore,' said Rosie.

'Ah. Sorry about that,' said Matt.

'Don't be – I'm not,' said Rosie with a shrug. Then, deciding that her nan would never forgive her if she didn't take the opportunity to gather as much gossip as possible, she turned the question right back on him. 'How about you?'

'None of the above,' said Matt, leaning against the doorframe and folding his arms. 'I haven't had the time.'

'Oh,' said Rosie. She'd rather lost the thread of the conversation the minute his arm muscles popped. That tee shirt was having a seriously hard time holding it together around those guns! The sight took her straight back to the hallway a few minutes ago, and the view she'd been treated to the moment she'd set foot inside Seabury House. 'Coffee?' she squeaked. 'Toast?'

Man, she needed to get a grip... of those arms!

NO! Think unsexy thoughts!

Toast crumbs... and... butter and... GAH!

Now she was fantasising about rubbing his muscles with butter!

'Yes please - to both!' said Matt.

'Wh… what?' she gasped.

'The coffee and toast?' said Matt, sounding amused.

'Oh, right, of course!' said Rosie, reaching for the cafetière. She started to spoon coffee from the pack she'd bought the previous day, though she managed to scatter at least half of it onto the worktop. For some reason, her hands weren't quite as steady as usual.

Taking a deep breath, Rosie grabbed the kettle and started to pour. Unfortunately, Matt chose that exact moment to shift from his position in the doorway. Momentarily distracted by his approach, Rosie missed the cafetière completely and sent a splash of scalding water right across the back of her free hand.

'Ow!' she squealed, plonking the kettle down and cradling her stinging hand to her chest.

'Show me!'

Somehow, Matt was suddenly at her side, and all the light-hearted humour had disappeared from his voice. He held out his hand for hers.

'It's fine,' she said automatically, even though it was

stinging something chronic.

'Rosie, show me your hand,' he said again.

Something about his stern, serious voice made Rosie relent. This wasn't a side to Matt she recognised... and she wasn't sure if it was the shock of the hot water or the tone of his voice that had turned her knees to jelly.

Matt glanced at the back of her hand. Then, taking her arm, he steered her straight towards the kitchen sink. Turning on the cold tap, he tested it briefly and then shoved her hand under the cool stream.

Rosie let out a sigh of relief as the cold water started to ease the sting a bit.

'Okay, I'm good,' she said, trying to pull away.

'Nope,' he said, still holding her wrist gently. 'You need to stay put for a few minutes at least!'

'Honestly, it's fine!' she laughed, letting out a little shiver that had nothing to do with the cold water sluicing over her hand and everything to do with Matt's large paw wrapped around her wrist. 'It was just a spot of hot water. Seriously, I—'

'Hush,' chuckled Matt as he turned her hand over so that he could examine it with expert care.

'What are you,' said Rosie, 'some kind of doctor?'

'Actually, yes,' said Matt, not taking his eyes off her hand. 'That's exactly what I am.'

'Give over,' laughed Rosie.

'I'm serious,' said Matt. 'Didn't you know?'

Rosie shook her head in surprise.

Never in a million years would she have guessed that Matt Pepper would take the time to train to become a doctor. Didn't that take years? He *had* to be joking. Sure, he'd always been bright enough… but he'd never had much in the way of patience… or interest when it came to schoolwork! The idea of him slogging away through medical school just didn't compute.

'Erm… wow, that's impressive,' she said.

Matt just shrugged. 'Right, keep your hand under the water while I make the coffee. I don't think you've done any real harm… it's a bit pink, but—'

'I'll live,' said Rosie.

She was feeling like a right plonker, making such a fuss over nothing. Still… at least it meant she'd gathered another little titbit about Matt. She had a feeling he might not have volunteered the information if she hadn't hurt herself.

Rosie couldn't wait to tell her Nan what Matt had made of himself. Of course, there was the added bonus that she'd got to witness his bedside manner first-hand!

Gah. Bedside!

An image of Matt wearing nothing but that blanket flashed through Rosie's mind again. Luckily, Matt had let go of her wrist and had moved across the kitchen to finish off the coffee.

'That'll do,' she said, turning off the tap and grabbing a dish towel to dry her hand. It was a bit sore, but nothing too bad. 'I'd… erm… better get on with things, I guess.'

'Oh no, you don't!' said Matt. 'I want to keep an eye on you for a couple of minutes… in case you go into shock.'

Rosie snorted. 'I hardly think—'

'Besides… didn't you promise me toast?' he added with a cheeky smile.

That did it. Her nan would have her guts for garters if she didn't seize the opportunity to feed him up a bit.

'Hungry, huh?' she said lightly, heading for the toaster.

'Starving. I feel like I've been asleep for a week,' he said.

'More like eighteen hours,' said Rosie.

'*What?!*' gasped Matt.

'Yep. It was about three o'clock in the afternoon when you arrived…' she trailed off and glanced up at the kitchen clock. Matt followed her gaze. It was just coming up to nine in the morning.

'Wow!' said Matt. 'That's the longest sleep I've had in years!'

'Sounded like you needed it,' said Rosie, thinking of the loud rumbles that had drifted down the stairs the previous day.

'Don't tell me I was snoring?' he said, raising an eyebrow.

'Okay,' she said with a small smile, 'I won't!'

Rosie piled toast onto a plate and placed it on the kitchen table, along with the pack of butter, a knife and a fresh pot of jam.

'Right, I'd better get on with things!' she said reluctantly.

'As long as those "things" include joining me for breakfast, then I completely agree!' said Matt, flopping down into a chair and pouring two large mugs of coffee. 'You still like two sugars?'

Rosie hesitated for a long moment and then sat down opposite him. 'I've cut down to one.'

'Blimey!' said Matt. 'Who are you, and what have you done with the sugar fiend I know and... erm...' He trailed off, looking awkward.

The unsaid L-word hung heavy in the air.

Rosie quickly cast around for something to say to let him off the hook. 'So... do you feel better for some sleep? You were pretty out of it yesterday.'

'Yeah,' said Matt, focussing more than was entirely normal on spreading butter right to the edges of his toast. 'Though I'd probably still be fast asleep if it wasn't for the phone call. Sorry about that, by the way...' said Matt.

Rosie shrugged and sipped her coffee, keeping her eyes on the table. 'It's fine.'

'No... I should have come to apologise straight away, but... well...' he paused and cleared his throat. 'I figured I'd better have a shower and find some clothes first!'

Rosie glanced at him and then froze. 'Ah shit, the shower!'

Matt raised his eyebrows in surprise. 'What

about it?'

'I completely forgot to buy new soap yesterday,' she said. 'I'm so sorry – I meant to grab some in town, but…'

But she'd forgotten it along with a whole bunch of other stuff – including spare loo roll. Unfortunately, the knowledge that Matt Pepper was taking a nap in his childhood bedroom had rather done a number on her concentration.

'It's fine,' chuckled Matt. 'I found an ancient bar in the dish and gave it a good scrub to bring it back to life!'

Rosie wrinkled her nose. 'I'm so sorry. I'll grab some fresh stuff today.'

'Erm… would you mind adding shampoo to the list?' said Matt. 'It's gone solid in the bottom of the bottle, and there's definitely no bringing that back to life!'

'Oh nooooo!' said Rosie, dropping her head into her hands. She could kick herself. At least she'd cleaned the various bathrooms and toilets, but decades-old soap and desiccated shampoo were unforgivable.

'Hey – there was a clean towel, so I'm not complaining!' chuckled Matt.

'Yeah, but Nan wouldn't have missed such an obvious thing,' sighed Rosie.

'Don't beat yourself up,' said Matt with a wicked grin. 'I mean… you're still in your probationary period!'

'Cheeky bugger!' muttered Rosie.

'And on that note, I can categorically say you're not in shock,' said Matt.

Rosie rolled her eyes at him and took a bite of buttery toast. 'So... what's the plan today? More napping?'

Matt shook his head. 'That was Charlie on the phone... apparently Lionel wants a word. I need to head down to the hotel... though I can't say I'm ecstatic about having to face Veronica Hughes on my first day back!'

'Veronica?!' laughed Rosie. 'You're safe there – she left town ages ago.'

'She did?' said Matt, looking relieved.

Rosie nodded. 'I wonder what Lionel's after...'

'No idea,' said Matt, grinning at her. 'For the record, that was such a Seabury thing to say.'

'Gotta gather as much gossip for Nan as I can,' said Rosie with a shrug, 'otherwise I'll be in trouble! She's starting to climb the walls, cooped up in the cottage.'

'In that case, walk down to town with me?' said Matt. 'It's Seabury... you never know what news you might pick up!'

Rosie paused, her coffee cup halfway to her lips. Was it *really* a good idea to spend so much time with Matt?

'Okay.' The word bypassed her brain and slipped out without her permission. 'I'd love to.'

CHAPTER 7

MATT

'Hey, wait up!'

Rosie puffed as she pelted across the garden, doing her best to catch up with him. Matt reluctantly slowed his stride. The sooner he reached the old door with its layer of flaking green paint, the sooner he could escape the grounds of Seabury House.

'Sorry,' he muttered, suddenly awkward.

Matt knew he was being a complete child, not waiting the few seconds it took for Rosie to lock the front door behind them, but the sight of the overgrown garden was doing something strange to him.

It was a beautiful day. Spring sunshine smiled down from an almost cloudless sky, and a light breeze carried the scent of salt and promises. But, rather than stirring up a sense of nostalgia, the brightness only served to highlight the disarray surrounding him. It was like a giant finger pointing out how he'd failed to look after the place.

Then again, the care of his childhood home wasn't just down to him – he *did* have three brothers – and Seabury House belonged to them all equally. But they'd been busy too… living their lives and avoiding the past.

Ewan, William and Rory all bore the same scars as Matt. But his brothers carried the extra damage he'd inflicted by practically demanding to be sent to boarding school just weeks after their father's death. Never in a million years had Matt expected their mother to do the same thing to his younger brothers.

Gah, he really needed to get out of there!

'You okay?' said Rosie, peering up at his face. 'You've gone all pale again - like yesterday. Are you sure you're up for a long walk?'

Matt nodded. 'A walk is exactly what I need.'

Anything to escape the memories flooding in.

His dad, lying on the grass…

Rosie, with tears rolling down her cheeks…

Leaving everything behind…

'Come on, let's get out of here,' he muttered.

'Lead the way!' said Rosie, shooting him a little frown.

Thankfully, she left it at that… but Matt wasn't fooled. The Rosie Phillips he knew was like a dog with a bone if she thought something was wrong. That was part of the reason he'd ended things with her all those years ago. He'd been heartbroken, and she would have made him talk about it. Talking was the last thing he'd wanted to do, even though it was probably what he'd needed most.

Logically, Matt knew it hadn't really been his fault. He'd been sixteen – and bound to explode at some point. Unfortunately, Rosie had been caught in the blast.

Sure, things were different now. Matt was an adult. He'd learned a lot. But he was well aware that his emotions were in freefall once more. The last thing he wanted was for Rosie to get caught in the crossfire again – like some sick echo of the past.

But... it was so good to have her close to him after all those years apart...

Yanking on the old door, Matt held it open for Rosie and then followed her onto the shaded, tree-lined path. The second he closed it behind them, he let out a sigh of relief. It would be a blessing to leave his mother's overrun flower beds and the lonely old house behind for a couple of hours.

'I... erm... I guess it's a lot?' said Rosie. 'Being home, I mean. Lots of memories?'

Matt smirked. *There it was! He didn't think she'd be able to wait long before giving him a little prod to find out what was wrong.*

'I'm fine,' he said. Then he sighed. This was Rosie... he might as well be honest with her. Otherwise, she'd just keep at it until she got to the bottom of what was bothering him.

'It's just… the house is so quiet… and seeing the garden like it is…'

Rosie nodded, waiting for him to continue.

'I just never imagined it'd all be in such a state!' he blurted.

Even as the words rushed out of him, Matt wanted to kick himself. It sounded like he was having a dig at Rosie and her Nan – and that was the last thing he meant to do. The fact that Seabury House was still standing and in one piece was down to the pair of them taking care of it!

'I'm sorry,' he said, turning to her. 'I didn't mean—'

'Hush!' she said with a smile. 'It's fine, I know what you meant.'

'Phew!' Matt paused. 'Okay… well, as long as you do. Because I'm so grateful to your Nan for looking after the house all these years—and you too, of course.'

'But you didn't expect it to have changed?' said Rosie, raising an eyebrow.

Matt nodded. She'd put her finger right on the sore spot.

'Exactly,' he said. 'It was like a kind of comfort blanket. I was convinced everything would be the same. The house… the gardens… the town. I thought Seabury would always be there—somewhere in the background—unchanged. It sounds stupid, but knowing that has kept me going.'

'It doesn't sound stupid at all,' said Rosie, moving to walk beside him as the path rounded a bend and widened out. 'I think we all have an anchor like that. Nan's mine. Sounds like Seabury House is yours?'

Matt nodded. 'I guess coming back has made me realise the heart of a place is all about the people—that's what made the town and Seabury House what it was—and that's not something I can ever get back.'

'Oh, I don't know about that,' said Rosie quietly.

Matt started as he felt her fingers lightly graze the back of his hand. It was only for a fleeting second, but the contact both electrified and calmed him all at once.

'You think?' he said, his voice low as it struggled around a lump of emotion.

'Well,' she said, 'I guess it depends on a few things.'

'Like what?' said Matt.

'Like… on how long you plan to stay,' said Rosie. 'You didn't say in your phone message. Or, if you did, that bit was garbled!'

'Honestly,' said Matt, 'I don't really know. I guess it depends on work…'

Even the thought of heading back to London—back to the busy GP practice—made him want to lie down in a darkened room.

'So, how did you become a doctor anyway?' said Rosie.

Matt blinked at the abrupt change of topic.

'Lots and lots of studying,' he laughed.

'I just can't imagine it!' she said, glancing at him. 'You never sat still long enough to study.'

'It's surprising what you can do when you put your mind to it,' he said, deliberately keeping his tone light.

It was amazing what you could do when you'd watched your dad die right in front of you, and you didn't have the first clue how to help him.

'Well, I think it's amazing,' said Rosie. 'I mean, we're talking years and years of training, aren't we?'

Matt nodded. It had been the perfect distraction.

'But... didn't you say you've been travelling?' she said. 'How does that work with the doctoring?'

'The travelling's part of it,' said Matt. 'I did a year's placement after my foundation programme—working with a charity to provide medical care in some of the poorest places you can imagine.'

'Wow,' said Rosie.

'It was... an eye opener,' said Matt. 'After I was fully qualified, I did several more stints, focusing on rural health programs. I wanted to make a lasting difference – and those were more about training local staff and improving care – as well as running clinics.'

'And that's what you've just come back from?' said Rosie.

Matt nodded, letting out a wide yawn.

'Well, no wonder you're knackered then!' she said, wide-eyed.

'I don't sleep well when I'm travelling,' he said, deciding to leave it at that for now.

It didn't feel like the right moment to mention some of the horrors he'd witnessed. The extreme poverty contrasting with the hope against all odds was inspiring and heartbreaking in equal measure. It always took him a while to adjust to the culture shock when he returned to the UK. This time, though, the bone-deep tiredness was on a whole other level.

'So… has your job given you some time off, then?' said Rosie.

'They gave me a sabbatical of sorts,' said Matt. 'The hospital where my practice is based gave me time to travel since they're partnered with the charity. I negotiated for a bit extra, though.'

'A bit?' said Rosie.

Matt nodded. What had he said to HR in the email he'd sent from the airport on his return? He was "re-evaluating his options."

Maybe after a break and some sleep, he'd be ready to head back to his day-to-day grind… but something deep inside told him it was time for a change. He just wasn't sure what that was going to look like yet.

'It's so strange you didn't even know I'm a doctor!' said Matt.

'Why?' laughed Rosie.

'I guess because it's all I've lived and breathed since I left town,' said Matt. 'And because I would've thought someone would have told you—your nan, Charlie… even Lionel!'

'If any of them knew you'd become a doctor,' she said, 'everyone else in town would have known to—including me.'

'Huh, weird,' said Matt.

'Why?' said Rosie, looking curious.

'Well, to be honest, I assumed Charlie called me this morning because Lionel needed a doctor,' he said. 'But... if they don't know...'

'Trust me, they don't,' said Rosie, with absolute certainty.

'Then I wonder what Lionel wants to talk to me about!' said Matt.

'Only one way to find out!' chuckled Rosie.

CHAPTER 8

ROSIE

'Well, I guess I better leave you to it then,' said Rosie as they came to a halt in front of the Pebble Street Hotel.

As she said it, her heart fell. She didn't want to say goodbye.

You're being ridiculous! It's only for a little while!

Rosie had enjoyed every second of the walk down from Seabury House... even if Matt's incredible drive and devotion to his job had made her feel like a bit of an underachiever. When he'd asked her what she'd been up to since they'd parted ways, it had been tough to stop herself from making excuses. But Rosie had learned a long time ago that she didn't have to have some kind of lofty goal to live a good life.

An amazing life, in fact.

Sure, the few serious relationships she'd been in hadn't lasted, and she didn't have many material possessions to show for her thirty years on the planet... but every day was an adventure full of old friends and small pleasures.

Sometimes, Rosie couldn't help but wonder if she was missing out on something... but as long as she lived in the moment, she was happy. She loved her Nan. She loved being back in Seabury. She loved spending time at Seabury House too. It was a wonderful old place... it just needed some company. With any luck, now that Matt was back—even if it was just for a little while—its fortunes might change.

'Earth to Rosie!'

Rosie blinked. Matt was busy waving one hand in front of her face as if he was trying to bring her out of a trance.

'Huh?'

'You completely zoned out!' he said. 'So... what do you think?'

'About what?' said Rosie. She'd definitely missed something.

'About coming into the hotel with me!' said Matt. 'Blimey, you really were miles away.'

'Sorry!' she said, trying to ignore the fact that her heart was doing a little tap dance with pleasure. 'Erm... are you sure that's a good idea?'

'Yeah, why not?' said Matt. 'From what you said earlier, Lionel doesn't know I'm a doctor, so it's not likely to be about anything medical. Besides, I could really do without putting my foot in it and I'm still half asleep and… pleeeeease?!' he ended on a whine.

'Okay, fine,' she laughed. 'I'll come and save you from yourself… but only because I want to see if Hattie's got any of her amazing pistachio pastries left over from breakfast.'

'Hattie?' said Matt.

'Lionel's niece… or… great niece,' said Rosie. 'Something like that, anyway. She's the head chef, and she's amazing!'

'Wait, Lionel's niece is head chef?' said Matt.

Rosie nodded.

'So, did she buy the place after Veronica left, then?' he said, looking confused.

'No, Lionel did!' said Rosie. 'Wait… didn't you know?'

Matt shook his head and ran his fingers through his hair, leaving behind little tufts that made him look adorably befuddled.

'See,' he said. 'I *need* you with me in there… I don't know anything anymore! Goodness knows what I might end up agreeing to… I'm totally going to put my foot in it!'

'Okay, breathe!' chuckled Rosie. 'Lionel's lovely. You know that. Unlike Veronica, I guarantee he's not out to get you!'

'Still, maybe we need a safe word,' muttered Matt. 'Just in case.'

'A safe word?!' hooted Rosie before clapping her

hand over her mouth and glancing around to check no one had overheard her. 'Why?!'

'So you can save me if I'm about to commit a major Seabury faux pas,' he said. 'You can cut me off at the pass.'

'Okay, fine,' said Rosie, shaking her head in amusement. 'In that case, if I say *blanket* – you know you've strayed into some kind of danger zone.'

'Blanket?' said Matt. 'Mean!'

'Ah come on,' she said with an evil grin, 'I'm not letting you forget about that for a *loooong* time.' Then, not wanting to give Matt enough time to digest what she'd just said, she gave him a gentle shove towards the hotel. 'Come on... I want to see if there's a second breakfast in the offing!'

As they stepped into the golden, gleaming light of the reception, the delicious scent of bacon, pastries and fresh coffee assailed their senses. Rosie lifted her nose in delight.

'I know we just had breakfast,' muttered Matt, glancing at her over his shoulder, 'but my stomach's rumbling!'

'That's the magic of Hattie's kitchen,' chuckled Rosie, putting her hand on her belly as it let out a plaintive groan of its own.

'Matt, my boy!'

They both turned to find Lionel unfolding like a friendly jack-in-the-box from behind the hotel's reception desk. 'And Rosie too, how lovely. Hattie told me you were back in town to look after Prudence.'

Rosie grinned at Lionel and gave him a sheepish little wave.

'Sorry... I hope you don't mind. I'm gate-crashing in the hope of purloining some pastries!'

Lionel smiled broadly. 'Of course I don't mind. It's lovely to see *both* of you... I remember you two when you were young scamps, walking hand-in-hand through town on your way to buy sweets from Doris.'

Rosie felt her cheeks grow pink, and she shot a glance at Matt.

'Long time ago,' murmured Rosie.

'Mmm,' said Lionel. 'Well, this must be serendipity at work because what I've got to say to Matt will affect you too.'

'Me?' said Rosie.

Lionel nodded. 'First things first, though. The guests are all in the dining room this morning, so why don't you two make yourselves comfortable in the breakfast room? I'll nip into the kitchen and ask Hattie if she's got any pastries left... unless you fancy a bacon sandwich?'

'Ooh, bacon?' said Matt.

'Let me see what I can do,' chuckled Lionel. 'Tea? Coffee?'

'Coffee please!' they both said in unison.

'I swear I just heard your stomach rumbling again,' said Rosie as Lionel beetled off towards the kitchen.

'Right back at you,' said Matt. 'Anyway, do you have any idea where the breakfast room is?'

'Sure,' said Rosie.

Her hand twitched, and it was as much as she could do to stop herself from reaching out and lacing her fingers through his. Instead, she shoved it determinedly into the pocket of her jeans. Edging around Matt, she led the way down the hall and into the cosy breakfast room.

By the time Lionel reappeared with a tray bearing three cups of coffee, the pair of them had settled silently into opposite ends of a squashy sofa.

Two seconds later, the door opened again to reveal a beaming Hattie.

'Ooh, it's the breakfast angel!' said Rosie. 'Hattie, I don't think you've met Matt before?'

Hattie shook her head as she placed a second tray on the low table in front of them. 'I don't think so… though I guess we might have met in passing when we were kids. I used to come down and stay with Uncle Lionel in the school holidays!'

'Seabury's the best place when you're a kid!' said Matt.

Rosie watched as a flicker of emotion crossed his face, and he picked up his cup of coffee and took a sip.

'This all looks amazing!' said Rosie quickly, wanting to give him a second to recover from whatever memory had just crash-landed.

'Pistachio pastries, just for you!' said Hattie,

handing her a plate piled with a pyramid of perfect miniature pastries. 'And here's a bag – I know they're your Nan's favourites too – take whatever's left over back home for her.'

'That's so kind of you,' said Rosie, shooting her a grateful smile. 'She'll be thrilled - thank you.'

'Lionel said the pair of you looked like you needed a mountain of bacon sandwiches, so I made you these.' She unloaded a stacked platter from the tray. 'Here's ketchup... brown sauce...'

'And vinegar?!' said Rosie.

'Ah – you'll have to forgive Uncle Lionel for that,' laughed Hattie. 'It's one of his little weirdnesses! Right... lovely to meet you, Matt, but I've got to dash.'

'Thank you!' said Matt, still sounding slightly dazed as Hattie disappeared.

'Tuck in!' said Lionel, nodding at the feast.

Rosie grabbed a napkin and one of the pastries. She nibbled off a delicious corner, and it was as much as she could do not to let out a whimper of pure delight.

'Now then,' said Lionel, 'I'm glad you're both here. I need to ask a huge favour... mainly from you, Matt... but you too, Rosie, if I'm honest.'

Rosie swallowed her mouthful of pastry. 'Me?' she said.

Lionel nodded. 'From what I understand, you've taken over from Prudence at Seabury House?'

'Temporarily,' said Rosie. 'Just until her hip's better.'

'I see,' said Lionel. 'Well, it's like this... Matt – I don't know if you're aware that I'm engaged?'

'Charlie told me yesterday,' said Matt, swallowing a mouthful of bacon sandwich. 'Congratulations.'

'Thank you,' said Lionel, inclining his head.

'Who's the lucky lady?'

'Mary Scott,' said Lionel. 'I believe you knew her back in the day.'

'Our old headmistress?' said Matt, raising his eyebrows.

'The very same,' said Lionel.

'Wow, you're a brave man.'

'I'm a *lucky* man,' said Lionel, with a twinkle in his eye. 'Trust me, boy, when the love of your life gives you a second chance – you grab it with both hands.'

Rosie, who'd been watching their exchange like a game of ping pong, shifted slightly. She'd think Lionel was talking about her and Matt if she didn't know any better. But her Nan had filled her in on Lionel and Mary Scott's epic love story. The woman in question was a formidable character, but apparently she'd softened a great deal since Lionel had proposed.

'Anyway, Mary's put her foot down,' said Lionel. 'She's refusing to have the wedding reception here at the hotel.'

'But why?' said Matt.

'It's your home!' said Rosie in surprise.

'Plus, it's gorgeous here!' said Matt.

'Thank you,' said Lionel. 'I think so too... though I'll

be spending most of my time at the Old School House after the wedding.'

'Hmm,' said Matt. 'Why do I get the feeling this has something to do with Veronica Hughes?'

'Ah, you remember her, do you?' said Lionel.

'Remember her?' laughed Rosie. 'He almost didn't come to see you because he thought she'd be here!'

'I don't blame you one bit, my boy—she was a terror,' said Lionel. 'Thankfully, she's long gone. But you're not wrong.' He paused and let out a long sigh. 'I'm afraid Mary's got some difficult memories associated with Veronica and her reign at Pebble Street.'

'Okay... I'm starting to see why Mrs Scott might want to celebrate her big day somewhere a bit more neutral,' said Rosie.

'It's understandable,' Lionel nodded. 'I could kick myself that I didn't winkle it out of her sooner. I've known for a while there's been something bothering her... but it only came out over the last couple of days. That's why I was so happy when Charlie told me you'd come home, Matt.'

'But... how can I help?' he said, looking nonplussed.

Rosie widened her eyes. Wasn't it obvious?!

Uh oh, she needed to give Matt the heads-up – before he blundered into something while he was half asleep!

Rosie wracked her brain, wondering how on earth she was going to work the word *blanket* into a sentence without sounding like a total psycho. Why couldn't she have chosen an easier word?!

Blanket! Blanket! Blanket!

'Well,' said Lionel, 'I guess there's no point beating about the bush. I was wondering if we could borrow Seabury House for the occasion.'

'Wow,' said Matt. 'Well, I'd be honoured. Of course you can use the house.'

Too late!

'Wow,' echoed Rosie. There was no backing out now… and she couldn't wait to see the look on Matt's face when he heard the full details!

'We're getting married in the registry office over in Dunscombe,' said Lionel, 'but we want something special for the reception. I was lucky enough to visit Seabury House when your parents lived there… it's the perfect spot.'

Rosie saw Matt's jaw tense at the mention of his parents.

'Glad to help,' he said, forcing a smile. 'And I'm sure Rosie or Mrs Phillips won't mind opening the place up for you…'

'But you're invited too, my boy!' said Lionel, beaming. 'Blimey – you'll be the guest of honour!'

'That's very kind,' said Matt. 'But there's a good chance I won't be staying long… maybe two or three weeks at most… I'm not sure yet.'

'That'll work a treat then,' said Lionel, looking delighted. 'The wedding's next weekend!'

CHAPTER 9

MATT

A wedding? Here? In a week and a half?
He was screwed!

Matt had been blinking in bewilderment ever since he'd left the Pebble Street Hotel, leaving a beaming Lionel in his wake.

He'd followed Rosie wordlessly around the shops as she'd picked up the bits and pieces she needed. Then she'd peered at him in concern before insisting they caught the bus back up the hill rather than walk. Matt had a feeling she'd somehow managed to persuade the driver to take a little detour in order to drop them right outside the grounds of Seabury House. He'd certainly never seen a bus stop this near the gates before!

Or maybe it was a new thing...

Either way, he wasn't complaining... he needed to sit down in a nice, dark corner!

'Matt?' said Rosie, following him through the gateway into the gardens. 'You okay? You've been practically silent since we left the hotel!'

Matt stared around at the overgrown garden, then up at the house. It looked decidedly scruffy and worn out in the bright sunshine.

He knew how it felt!

'Matt?' There was rising concern in Rosie's voice now. 'Have I done something wrong?'

'You?' said Matt, turning to look at her. 'Definitely not.' He shook his head, doing his best to ignore the heavy carrier bag full of shopping intent on walloping him in the kneecaps with every move he made. 'That said, we *did* have a safe word… and you didn't use it… so I guess I *could* blame you for this mess!'

Rosie's eyebrows shot up. 'You've lost me.'

'Blanket!' he squeaked, aware that he probably sounded a tad deranged. 'Why didn't you *blanket* the living daylights out of me the minute Lionel mentioned his wedding?!'

'Because—' Rosie started, but Matt wasn't done.

'Gah… what have I done?!' he muttered. 'How on earth am I meant to host a wedding reception here in less than two weeks' time? The place is a dump!'

'Take a—' Rosie tried again.

'I'll call Lionel and tell him I've made a mistake,' he said, cutting across her again. 'I've got to, haven't I? There's no other option, is there? What do you think?'

Rosie stared at him in silence.

'What?' he said, feeling the anxiety swirl around him. 'Say something!'

'Just making sure you were all *panicked-out* first,' she said with a smirk.

Matt widened his eyes, realising he'd just word-vomited all over her without taking a breath. 'Sorry,' he muttered, miming zipping his lips.

'It's fine,' said Rosie, smiling at him.

The familiar sight was as comforting as a hug, and he breathed a little easier.

'To answer your most *excellent* points…' she paused and took a deep breath. 'No, I don't think you made a mistake, and no, I don't think you should call Lionel to cancel. Yes, it *might* have been a good idea to wait until you had all the details before agreeing to it… and yes, I *should* have given you the heads-up that you were about to jump in with both size… tens?' she glanced down at his feet.

'Elevens,' he muttered. 'So… why didn't you?!'

'You try working the word "blanket" into a conversation with no warning,' she huffed. 'It's practically impossible.'

'You chose it,' said Matt.

'It was my first time picking a safe word,' said Rosie. 'Next time, I'll choose something a bit easier to blurt!'

Matt glared at her for a long moment, and then a strange bubble rose up his throat, and a giggle escaped. He hiccupped, snorted, and clapped his hand over his mouth… but nothing helped. His shoulders started to shake as the ridiculousness of the situation crashed over him.

It took all of two seconds for Rosie to join in, and before long, the pair of them were bent double. She reached out and clasped his shoulder to steady herself.

'Why are we l-l-l-aughing?!' wheezed Rosie.

'Blanket!' giggled Matt. 'Blanket!' He tried to suck in a calming breath. It didn't help. His tiredness and anxiety had just morphed into a puddle of hysteria... and Rosie Phillips was right where she belonged –at his side, egging him on.

It took a good five minutes before the pair of them managed to straighten up properly and stop dissolving every time one of them tried to speak.

'What I want to know,' said Rosie, deliberately avoiding making eye contact with him, 'is why on earth you were so quick to agree?! I mean... the house has been closed up for years.'

Matt shrugged. 'I got swept up in the romance of the thing!'

'Softy!' laughed Rosie.

'And I kind of assumed we'd have ages to sort something out...' he sighed. 'Or... that's what I *would* have assumed if I'd given it any thought!'

The scale of the favour he'd just agreed to was busy bopping him over the head again. Of course, he'd vaguely taken in the state of the garden when he'd arrived the previous evening - and when he'd made his break for it that morning - but now they were back from town, the encroaching brambles and the weather-battered façade of his childhood home looked a hundred times worse.

'What have I done?!' he sighed as the remaining humour drained out of him, only to be replaced with tiredness again. 'The place doesn't exactly scream "wonderful wedding reception", does it?'

Rosie cocked her head and stared up at the house. 'I do see your point,' she said. 'And I'm guessing Lionel hasn't been here in… what… about twenty years?'

'Sounds about right,' said Matt, nodding. 'Being a kid, I never really thought about it, but I suppose the place was pretty grand back then…'

'Apart from the four hellions bounding around, riding skateboards down the halls and building dens in the gardens?' laughed Rosie.

'Make that five hellions,' he said, pointing at her.

'I stand corrected!' she said.

Matt glanced around the garden again, doing his best not to be swallowed by a wave of guilt. How could he have let it get in this state when it had been such a refuge for them as kids? Seabury House, with its vast rooms, sprawling gardens, and high wall had provided them with total safety and freedom. It had been an amazing place to spend his childhood… and he'd just turned his back on it.

'What am I going to do?' he said, rubbing his face.

'Yeah – it's going to be a major undertaking,' she nodded.

'Gee, thanks for your support!' he said.

'I'm just telling it like it is,' she said, shooting him a cheeky wink.

'So much for a few weeks of rest and recuperation,' said Matt. 'I don't suppose you happen to know anyone with a bulldozer?'

'You know, I think you're looking at this all wrong,' said Rosie, folding her arms. 'This is Seabury. I bet we'd find plenty of people willing to help out if we asked around.'

'We?' he said, looking at her hopefully. 'You're up for giving me a hand? I mean... I *did* land myself in this mess...'

'Of course I'm up for it!' said Rosie. 'You can't get rid of me that easily. And like I say – I bet plenty of other people would be up for the challenge too.'

'As much as I love your positivity, I doubt many people in town even remember me,' said Matt. 'Even if they do, I can't expect them to give up their time to come all the way up here to help me.'

'You're underestimating a couple of key things,' said Rosie, squaring her shoulders and looking scarily like she was ready for action.

'Which are...?' he said.

'Number one – just how popular Lionel and Mary are,' said Rosie. 'If the happy couple want Seabury House wedding-ready in less than two weeks, it'll happen.'

'It's going to take a miracle,' said Matt.

'Well, at least that's something Seabury's good at providing,' said Rosie.

'What, miracles?' said Matt.

Rosie nodded.

'What's the second thing I'm underestimating?' said Matt.

'Just how nosy people are,' she said. 'No one's been inside these walls for years—other than me, Nan and that plumber who had to come and stop the downstairs loo from impersonating a fountain.'

Matt wrinkled his nose. 'You seriously think we'll get enough people up here to help sort things out just because they want to have a nose around?!'

'I'd bet on it,' said Rosie.

Matt took a deep breath and nodded slowly. There was still a good chance she was being overly optimistic, but Rosie's can-do attitude was starting to part his swirling clouds of worry. The house might not be too bad, but it was going to take more than a bit of elbow grease to get the garden presentable in such a short space of time. Still, if Rosie was right and they could drum up a small army of willing volunteers… it might just about be possible.

'Question is, where do we start?' he said.

'Charlie,' said Rosie firmly. 'If *anyone* can find a way to sort this place out in time for Lionel's wedding, it's him.'

CHAPTER 10

ROSIE

'Hello, hello – anyone home?' Rosie called, approaching the little shed towards the back of Charlie's allotment plot.

No answer.

Rosie sighed. She wasn't entirely sure why she'd volunteered to go on the hunt for their saviour when it came to the newly dubbed *Great Wedding Plan*. It could have been something to do with the fact that she was feeling a bit guilty.

After they'd recovered from their joint bout of hysterics earlier on, Rosie had insisted on dragging Matt through Seabury House, making sure that he had a look in every single room.

It was all well and good being the optimistic one when it came to their ridiculously tight deadline. Still, Rosie had decided it was important to be honest with Matt about how much work lay ahead of them. She realised he'd barely seen more than the kitchen, his bedroom, and one of the bathrooms since coming home.

In the name of transparency, Rosie had insisted on towing him through the house—throwing open curtains and yanking dustsheets from piles of disused furniture as she went. In hindsight, maybe ripping the plaster off like that wasn't the best idea.

By the time they'd completed the full tour and returned to the kitchen for a well-earned cup of tea, Matt had turned an interesting shade of putty. He'd looked like he was in desperate need of a nap. After a bit of prodding—and a promise that she'd return first thing in the morning—Rosie convinced him to head upstairs to bed. It hadn't taken much effort.

Even now, standing among the well-ordered vegetable plots, Rosie's thoughts were still back in Seabury House with Matt. She was worried about him. He might be all tall, tanned and toned, but there were dark circles underneath his eyes, and his tendency to zone out hinted at something more worrying than the need to catch up on a bit of sleep.

A prickle of fear ran down Rosie's spine.

What if he was ill?

She shook her head, instantly dismissing the thought. Matt was a busy doctor, and he clearly pushed himself to the limits when it came to his stints abroad with the charity. Still... she'd be keeping a close eye on him while he was in town! At least the Great

Wedding Plan had one silver lining—it gave her the perfect excuse to spend plenty of time at the house with him.

For his wellbeing, of course... it had nothing to do with the weird, magnetic pull she felt whenever she was near him.

Now she just needed to keep her fingers crossed that Matt didn't get cold feet and call the whole thing off while she wasn't around to stop him in his tracks. All the more reason to find Charlie and rope him into the plan asap! Between them, they might be able to summon a bit of Seabury spirit—anything to show Matt he wasn't on his own.

'Question is... where *is* Charlie?!' she muttered, stripping off her light jacket and tying the arms around her waist.

Rosie had decided to start her search there as it was usually a good bet he'd be working away on his beloved plot somewhere. The man practically lived there... or at least, he had done before Ethel had put a ring on him.

'If he's not here... he's either at The Sardine or cosied up in Ethel's kitchen!' sighed Rosie. She *really* didn't fancy the walk all the way back down into town again.

'First sign of madness, you know!'

It was Charlie – she'd know that voice anywhere! With a broad grin, Rosie turned, searching for his familiar face – only to spot him emerging over the brow of the hill.

'What is?' she laughed. 'Talking to myself or visiting the allotments?'

'Cheeky blighter!' chuckled Charlie. He drew a grubby handkerchief from the breast pocket of his checked shirt and mopped his forehead 'Blimey, tis warm for the time of year!'

'I know!' Rosie said, pointing to the jacket slung around her waist. 'I've already had to shed a layer.'

'You should see what it's like in Ben's polytunnel!' he puffed. 'I've just been down there to open it up for him so that his seedlings don't get baked!'

'At least there's a bit of a breeze up here,' said Rosie, eyeing the old deckchair outside Charlie's shed with longing.

'If you're not in a hurry, feel free to pull up a pew!' said Charlie, 'I can't offer you anything cold, but I can do you a cuppa if you fancy?'

'That would be brilliant, thanks!' said Rosie. 'And I'm definitely not in a hurry – I came to see you!'

'Wonderful,' said Charlie, looking thrilled. 'What a treat.'

Opening the shed, he pulled out a spare deckchair and unfolded it with a flourish. 'There we go. Grab a seat while I fetch my flask!'

Rosie sank gratefully into the chair, and two seconds later, Charlie handed her a tin mug filled with a strong, tar-like brew. Then he fetched a large, round cake tin from the shed before settling gingerly onto the second deckchair.

'Can I tempt you?' he said, yanking the lid off and waving a smorgasbord of sugary delights in her direction.

Rosie leaned forward for a better look. There was everything from chocolate brownies to doughnuts to delicately iced sugary biscuits. Her mouth instantly started to water even though she'd already stuffed herself with Hattie's pistachio pastries.

'These Ethel's?' she said, struggling to choose between the treats.

'Of course,' laughed Charlie. 'I wouldn't be cheating on her with someone else's baking!'

'In that case, how can I say no to one of her brownies?' said Rosie, helping herself to a chocolatey chunk.

'Good choice… though I started the day with one of those, so it's a bit of Dorset apple cake for me this time, I think!' said Charlie, balancing a gooey piece of cake on one knee. 'Now then, to what do I owe the pleasure?'

'It's about that meeting you set up between Matt and Lionel,' she said. 'Matt roped me in too… for moral support.'

'Oh good!' said Charlie. 'That means you can fill me in on what happened. Did he agree?'

'He did,' said Rosie.

Matt's shell-shocked, panicked face swam in front of her for a moment.

'Excellent,' said Charlie with a nod of satisfaction.

'Mary will be much happier celebrating her big day at Seabury House. Don't get me wrong, the hotel's a fine place, but there are too many memories of vicious Veronica there for her to deal with on such a special occasion.'

'Yes, I get that…' said Rosie. 'But… can't you see the problem?'

'Problem?' said Charlie, raising his bushy eyebrows. 'Not as I can see.'

'With the house, I mean,' said Rosie. 'It's been empty for years. Decades, in fact!'

'As long as the place hasn't fallen down, I'm sure it'll be fine,' said Charlie stoutly. 'It's got good bones.'

'Yeah, but…' Rosie trailed off.

'Spit it out!' laughed Charlie.

'It's a lovely place, and Nan's done her best with it over the years, but…' she paused again.

'But?' prompted Charlie.

'Inside, it's a bit dusty, a bit grubby… and… lifeless?' she said, feeling like she was betraying an old friend.

'I'm sure it just needs a little TLC,' said Charlie.

'TLC?' said Rosie faintly. 'I haven't even told you about the garden yet. The brambles are closing in, the flower beds are gone… and don't even mention the words "wedding photos" because, in its current state, that's a total no-go.'

'Ah,' said Charlie. 'Well… that *is* a minor snag, I'll grant you. And Matt still went ahead and agreed?'

'He said he got swept up in the romance of it all,'

said Rosie with a small smile. 'You should have seen his face when we got back to the house and he realised what he'd let himself in for. I thought he was going to pass out for a minute!'

'Poor lad,' tutted Charlie. 'Seems he's a bit wrung out at present.'

'You could say that,' said Rosie.

'Well, no problem,' he said, popping a bit of cake into his mouth and savouring it. 'We just need to band together to get it sorted out in time for the wedding.'

Rosie let out a sigh of relief. 'It's so good to hear you say that, Charlie, because that's exactly what I came to see you about – to beg you for your help.'

'No need to beg,' chuckled Charlie. 'I'd do anything for Lionel—he's my best friend in the whole world. I'm sure there are plenty of other people who'll be keen to come along too.'

'You think?' said Rosie, crossing her fingers.

'Think?' said Charlie. 'I know it for a fact. Plenty of folks have been wanting to see inside those walls for years – me included! Give them the chance to have a nosy around Seabury House, and they'll be there like a shot.'

'That sounds… perfect,' said Rosie, letting out a sigh of relief.

'Well, we might not get the place perfect,' said Charlie, cocking his head, 'but between us, we'll make sure it's fit for a wedding! I'm glad Matt agreed –

though I'm not surprised. He's always been a good lad... in fact, they all were.'

'That's not quite how I remember it,' laughed Rosie. 'The Pepper brothers were feral – especially when they were in pack formation!'

'Ah, don't give me that,' laughed Charlie. 'You were quite keen on young Matt back in the day.'

Back in the day? She wasn't sure there was anything quite so past tense about how she felt about Matt.

'Has he told you much about what his brothers are up to?' said Charlie. 'They were all as bright as each other. Our Matt's a doctor, I hear? I wonder what the other boys made of themselves!'

'He didn't say,' said Rosie. In fact, it felt very much like Matt changed the subject any time she strayed anywhere near the topic of his family. 'You met him off the bus, didn't you?'

Charlie nodded. 'Pretty much.'

'Did he mention his brothers to you at all?' she said.

'He skirted right around that question!' Charlie shook his head and sighed. 'I've got a feeling those boys have drifted apart since they left Seabury.'

'Mmm,' said Rosie. 'And did you notice anything at all... *off*... about Matt?'

'Off?' said Charlie, his eyebrows bristling.

'I mean, he didn't seem... ill?' said Rosie. 'Or tired?'

'Oh, the lad was bone-tired!' said Charlie, nodding. 'Said as much himself, too. Just back from his travels, from what I gather, so it's not surprising.'

Rosie wondered how much Matt had told Charlie about his work with the charity. She'd love nothing more than to wax lyrical about how amazing he was for using his skills like that… but promptly decided it wasn't her story to tell.

'Well… I don't reckon he's ill,' said Charlie. 'I'm no doctor, mind, but my guess is that the lad's run himself ragged. I'd bet you anything he's not stopped to take a breath since he left town when he was a youngster.'

'You might be right,' said Rosie.

'Nothing a bit of time at home won't fix,' said Charlie.

'I'm not even sure how long he's planning to stay,' said Rosie. 'I don't think he knows either if I'm honest. He vaguely mentioned two or three weeks to Lionel, but I reckon he's just as likely to up and leave before then if things get too much.'

'Well, let's just make sure they don't then, eh?' said Charlie. 'We'll make sure he gets all the help he needs. Are you up for it, lass?'

'Oh, definitely,' said Rosie.

'Well then, I'll make some calls and gather a few folk, and we'll come up to the house tomorrow and see what's what,' said Charlie. 'We'll make a list – then we'll divide and conquer.'

CHAPTER 11

MATT

Matt stared at Rosie as she gathered her hair into a ponytail, doing his best not to get mesmerised by the glistening golden lights that danced wherever the sun touched the strands.

'Right, are you ready?' she said, scrambling up from the kitchen table and shooting a grin at him.

Matt nodded, amused by her barely contained excitement. Rosie was bouncing on the balls of her feet, clearly ready to tackle the challenge ahead. *This* was the Rosie he remembered. Always full of life and energy – ready for whatever adventure the day threw her way.

Matt had to admit, he'd been thoroughly relieved when she'd turned up not long after he'd made his way downstairs that morning. A nagging voice in the back of his mind had been whispering that she might have changed her mind about helping him now that she'd had a night to reconsider.

Slurping down the last mouthful of his coffee and getting to his feet, Matt gave her a decided nod. 'I'm ready!'

At least he could say that with all honesty today.

Matt had bounded out of bed for the first time in as long as he could remember. His second night's sleep in Seabury seemed to have had a much better effect than the first. Of course, it may have helped that he hadn't been rudely awakened by the ancient landline. Instead, he'd been greeted by the sweet sound of a robin singing lustily outside his bedroom window. He'd opened his eyes to find spring sunshine edging into his room around the curtains. It was a recipe for an instant good mood... Matt only wished he could bottle it for when he had to return to real life.

'Right, where should we start?' he said.

'Let's get one thing clear,' said Rosie, her tone mock-stern as she folded her arms and tapped her foot. 'Just because I'm the housekeeper, it doesn't mean I have to come up with all the plans. Got that, Dr Pepper?'

Matt let out a snort of amusement and gave her a quick nod. She did have a point... and she'd already gone above and beyond by heading off in search of Charlie and roping him in. Finding Rosie at Seabury House might have been a bit of a shock at first, but he couldn't think of anyone he'd rather face the upcoming chaos with!

'Okay, I promise to pull my weight,' said Matt.

Rosie was staring into the middle distance, clearly not listening.

'Waaaait!' she gasped. 'Dr Pepper!'

Matt gritted his teeth and rolled his eyes.

Here it comes!

'Oh. Em. GEE!!' she squealed. 'How the hell did you make it through medical school in one piece with that name?!'

'Don't even go there,' he sighed.

'Why?' chuckled Rosie. 'Don't tell me it's because you're *so missuuuunderstood?*' She sang the last few words, echoing the fizzy pop advert that had plagued him throughout his career.

'You know you're showing your age, don't you?' he said with a wry smile.

'You're four months older than me... so *there!*' Rosie stuck her tongue out at him. 'And I'm guessing that's not the first time someone's sung that jingle at you?'

'Try every single time I walked into a lecture theatre, the student union, the canteen... my graduation!' said Matt. 'I did get an awful lot of free cans of the stuff, though. People thought it was hilarious to pop them in my bag, on my desk and outside my dorm room door. I developed quite a taste for it in the end!'

'Not all bad, then,' laughed Rosie. 'Anyway... sorry... I couldn't resist.'

'I'll let you off,' he said with a shrug. 'Just this once!'

'Too kind,' she said with a little bow. 'Now then... where do *you* want to start, as it's *your* house?'

'Well, as Charlie's planning on turning up later – hopefully with some helpers... I'm hoping he'll be up for tackling the situation outside,' said Matt. 'So I guess we need to start inside the house.'

'Good call,' said Rosie. 'It might be beautiful weather out there now, but we can't bank on that happening on the big day.'

'Right,' said Matt. 'So... perhaps we should start with the main room Lionel and Mary will want to use for the celebrations and go from there.'

'Sounds like a solid plan,' said Rosie with a nod. 'The question is, with two sitting rooms, a dining room and a reception room... which one do you think Lionel and Mary might like to use?'

Matt cast his mind back to the whistle-stop tour around the house Rosie had insisted on the previous day.

'I've been thinking about this,' said Matt. 'It's got to be the ballroom, hasn't it?!'

'Nice,' said Rosie, nodding.

The ballroom was what they'd called the large reception room when they were kids. It had enormous windows that looked out over the south lawn... which was probably more like a wilderness right now. Hopefully, Charlie might be able to do something about that, though. No matter what time of day it was, light streamed into the ballroom, and it was easily large enough to host Lionel and Mary's reception.

'Only one drawback,' said Matt. 'That room's the main dumping ground!'

'And the one room Nan's not been able to clean properly for years because it's so crammed with stuff.' Rosie grabbed his hand and started tugging him out of the kitchen. 'Come on, let's go have a proper look.'

She towed him down the hallway and flung open the door.

'After you!' said Matt.

Rosie grinned at him and pulled him into the vast room without dropping his hand. They stood side-by-side in the dust-filled silence, taking it all in.

What had once been a grand, formal sitting room was now a cluttered graveyard of furniture and cardboard packing boxes. It was the one room Rosie hadn't been able to remove all the dust sheets from the previous day because it would have taken a serious bit of mountaineering to reach them all.

Patches of the wonderful old wooden floorboards were still visible here and there between the piles, and the sight of them made Matt smile. As far as he could remember, the ballroom had never actually hosted any balls, but it *had* been a great place for sliding on his knees from one end of the room to the other and ending up in a pile of fists and elbows with his brothers. He doubted the wedding guests would want to slide around on their knees... but it *was* the perfect place to host the reception.

'This is going to take a looooot of work!' he murmured, staring at the heaps of boxes, and the sleeping furniture tucked up beneath the dust sheets.

Rosie gave his hand a gentle squeeze. 'How about we start by uncovering everything, then we can go from there?'

Matt nodded. He could only vaguely remember what furniture had originally been in this room, so he wasn't sure what they were about to rediscover. He knew he was probably being daft, but there was a little bubble of apprehension hovering in his chest. How was he going to react when they got going? After all, this was his past they were about to rummage through... and it was a seriously long time since he'd come face to face with it!

'Come on,' said Rosie, rubbing her hands together. 'Race you to the other side of the room!'

Matt nodded and headed for the nearest dust sheet. It felt good to get going. He grinned as he whisked the dusty coverings from a huddle of six wooden dining chairs. 'These are the ones we used to drape blankets over for dens! One of them has a big dent in the leg where Rory pushed Ewan into it face first!'

'I remember that!' chuckled Rosie, who was already in the middle of an Olympic-worthy stretch across a pile of boxes on the other side of the room. 'He had an epic black eye, didn't he?'

Matt nodded. 'Yep. Mum went ballistic!'

'You must miss your brothers,' said Rosie.

'Mmm,' said Matt. *Damnit, he only had himself to blame for the conversation heading straight towards that question!* 'What time did you say Charlie might rock up?'

'You did it again!' huffed Rosie, straightening up and turning to stare at him. 'Every time I mention your brothers, you do an about-face-turn! What am I missing?'

'Nothing,' Matt shrugged. 'We just don't see much of each other these days, that's all.'

'Matt Pepper, don't make me come over there!' said Rosie, her voice so stern it made him smile in spite of himself. 'Don't forget you're talking to someone who's known you since… well… forever. I know when you're lying! Come on – spill – what's the big mystery?'

Matt shook his head. 'It's not a big deal.'

'It's clearly a big deal to you,' said Rosie, more gently, as she folded a dust sheet and tossed it to one side. 'Tell me – it might help.'

'I will… but later, if that's okay?' he said. He'd never told anyone before. The idea of admitting he was to blame for their idyllic family life at Seabury House coming to such an abrupt end was too much to face - especially while he was up to his knees in reminders of the past.

'Of course it's okay,' said Rosie softly. 'I mean… do you even know what they're doing these days?'

Matt sighed. There it was again – Rosie's stubborn need to help.

'Rory's a pilot,' he said.

'He's a *what?!*' gasped Rosie.

'He flies planes,' said Matt with a snort.

'Alright, smarty pants, I was just surprised that your baby brother has such a grown-up job!' said Rosie.

'He loves it,' said Matt. 'He's never in the country long enough to meet up... even if he wanted to.'

'What about Ewan?'

Matt grinned. As a kid, Ewan had always been the underachiever of the family - which was just ridiculous, considering he was now basically an Arctic explorer.

'Well,' said Matt, 'the last I heard, he'd just lost half a foot to frostbite in the Arctic. Or... maybe it was a toe... I never quite got to the bottom of it. For someone who spends most of his life around research scientists, he's remarkably vague with the details.'

'Blimey,' said Rosie, pulling a face. 'I don't fancy that much. A stiff wind over North Beach is enough to give me goosebumps.'

'I have to admit I don't fancy the sound of it much either,' said Matt.

'You've travelled loads, though,' said Rosie.

'Yeah,' said Matt, 'but wherever I go tends to be hot-to-roasting! No chance of frostbite.' Plenty of chances for lots of other nasties, but he did his best not to think about that too much.

'And what about William?' asked Rosie.

'William? He's a mystery!' laughed Matt. 'You basically have to call his agent if you want to stand any chance of tracking him down. I haven't spoken directly to him for years now. He hops from continent to continent – concert hall to concert hall.'

'Wait, concert hall?' said Rosie, looking intrigued.

'He's a pianist,' said Matt. 'A ridiculously good one—which is hilarious, considering none of the rest of us has a musical bone in our bodies.'

'Amen to that,' said Rosie. 'I'm still not over your attempt to play the clarinet.'

'Yeah, it was about as short-lived as your stint with the violin,' chuckled Matt. 'You sounded like a bag of cats!'

'Charming!' huffed Rosie. 'You know, I honestly don't think I ever heard Will play. I just remember him doing his best to get out of every single lesson whenever the music teacher visited school.'

'Yeah, for good reason,' laughed Matt. 'Turns out he was bored stiff. Will outgrew that teacher in just a few months! In the end, he had to come clean and tell Mum and Dad that he was basically teaching the teacher! And I'm not surprised you didn't hear him practise – he used to be weirdly private about it. He'd sneak down here after everyone else was in bed and play for hours. It sounded like the place was haunted by a very musical ghost!'

'Wait... he practised in here?' said Rosie, staring

around. 'Did your mum sell the piano before she moved?'

'I don't think so,' said Matt. 'No – see, over there – near the far wall.'

'Let's take a peep!' said Rosie.

It took the pair of them several minutes to shift enough boxes to carve a path towards the hulking mass near the windows, covered with two vast dust sheets.

'On three?' said Rosie, grabbing the corner of one of them.

'Okay – three!' said Matt, tugging at the other one.

A shiny black baby grand appeared in all its long-forgotten glory.

'Ooh,' said Rosie, dropping onto the padded stool. Matt watched as she lifted the lid and gingerly touched the ivory keys.

'Ouch!' he laughed. 'I haven't got perfect pitch like Will, but even I can tell that's out of tune.'

'It's still got a lovely tone, though, hasn't it?' said Rosie, playing a few halting, discordant scales.

Matt nodded. 'Well, there's no chance we'll be able to shift this out of the room for the wedding.'

'Why would you want to?' said Rosie. 'It'll make a great focal point and look gorgeous as a backdrop for some photos.'

'As long as no one tries to play it!' said Matt, pulling a face as Rosie hit another chord that set his teeth on edge. 'Hey, how do you fancy taking a break?'

'Already?' laughed Rosie. 'Dr Pepper – you're a terrible skiver. We've only just started!'

'Yeah, but the sun's out, and I could do with a cuppa and some fresh air,' said Matt.

And a little break from all the memories.

CHAPTER 12

ROSIE

The pair of them trudged out onto the weedy gravel with their arms full of dust sheets.

'What's wrong with you?' laughed Rosie, glancing over at Matt as she dropped her load in an unceremonious heap. His nose was screwed up, and he looked like he was in pain.

'I'm going to sn… sn…'

Matt didn't get to finish his sentence before he let out an almighty sneeze.

'I blame you!' he huffed, straightening up and sniffing.

'Well, for goodness sake, put them down!' she chuckled.

Rosie had insisted they should remove all the discarded sheets before they had a break for a cuppa. At least that way, when they got back to work in the ballroom, they would have taken one tiny step forward.

She watched as Matt dumped his armful on top of hers. A visible plume of dust rose from the pile, and she wrinkled her nose. It was a stark reminder of how much work lay ahead of them.

'Tell me honestly,' said Matt, 'do you really think we've got any chance of sorting that mess out in time for the wedding?'

Rosie straightened her spine and met his eyes. She didn't want to be the one to add any kind of doubt to proceedings. The job was tough enough already, but she had a feeling the emotional toll was going to make it even harder for Matt. He might have filled her in on what his brothers were up to, but there was definitely more to that story.

'Your silence isn't filling me with confidence here,' said Matt with a small smile.

Rosie caught a flurry of movement behind him.

'Sorry,' she said, breaking into a grin. 'I just got distracted. In answer to your questions – yes – I *definitely* think we've got a chance of being ready in time for the wedding!'

'What makes you so sure?!' said Matt, looking surprised.

In answer, Rosie raised her hand and pointed behind him.

'What?' said Matt, looking confused as he turned on the spot. Then he gasped.

Talk about good timing!

The old front gates had just been flung open, and

there stood Charlie at the head of a vast group of chattering people.

'Blimey!' said Matt.

'The cavalry has arrived,' said Rosie.

'I thought we'd be lucky if he managed to round up one or two helpers,' said Matt. 'I don't even recognise half of them.'

'It looks like he's gathered everyone from the allotments, most of the WI…' said Rosie.

'And even your Nan!' said Matt with a broad smile, raising his hand and waving like an excited little boy.

The minute Rosie spotted her grandmother in the crowd—with her hand wrapped around the crook of Charlie's elbow—she breathed a sigh of relief.

If there was anyone she wanted by her side when it came to feeding and watering this bunch of ragamuffins who'd just turned up for a glimpse of Seabury House, it was Prudence. Rosie was already wondering if there were enough clean cups in the kitchen, let alone if the couple of packets of Rich Tea biscuits she'd bought the previous day would stretch far enough.

'Mrs. Phillips!'

Matt's cry of joy as he rushed forward to take her Nan's hand brought Rosie back from her biscuit-related worries, and she practically melted on the spot.

Her Nan smiled at Matt with pure joy as she reached up to give his cheek a gentle pat.

'It's Prudence, Matt,' she said. 'Prudence.'

'You'll always be Mrs Phillips to me,' laughed Matt, taking her arm and leading her slowly towards the house as Rosie hurried to join them.

'Nan,' she gasped. 'You should be putting your feet up!'

'Don't fuss, girl,' chuckled Prudence. 'When Charlie came to the cottage to tell me what you were up to, there was no way I was going to miss out.'

'Well, having this many hands to help will certainly make things easier,' laughed Matt.

Rosie nodded enthusiastically.

'Now, don't you two get too excited,' said Prudence, lowering her voice so that the chattering crowd behind them wouldn't be able to hear. 'You know that lot are mainly here to rubberneck, right?'

'What do you mean?' said Matt.

Rosie widened her eyes at her Nan and gave her head a little shake. Convincing Matt that getting Seabury House wedding-ready was even within the realms of possibility was hard enough. The last thing she needed was for her Nan to add to his worries!

'Well,' said Prudence, completely ignoring Rosie's silent attempt to stop her in her tracks, 'your place has been a mystery in town for years. I think this lot are just curious to see what's inside the walls. Whether they're willing to roll their sleeves up and help get the job done remains to be seen.'

'Oh,' said Matt, his face falling.

'Well then,' said Rosie, deciding she'd better step in

before Matt retreated for a nap in a darkened room again, 'why not give them exactly what they want! Give them a tour, Matt—I bet you anything they'll all want to muck in and help once they've seen the place!'

'That's a great idea,' said Prudence, her eyes shining.

'Do you think?' said Matt.

He turned to peer at the chattering crowd. Several of them were poking around the flower beds. A few had wandered towards the far corner of the house, clearly keen to take a look at the gardens beyond. The rest were still standing with Charlie, watching Matt with eager eyes.

'Looks like you're right,' he said, sounding nervous. 'Okay – I'll take everyone on a tour. Do you want to join us, Prudence?'

'Nope.' Rosie's Nan shook her head. 'I know every inch of that house like the back of my hand already. Rosie and I will head into the kitchen to get things sorted out in there.'

'Oh, we will, will we?' laughed Rosie.

'Yes,' Prudence nodded firmly. 'We will.'

'Well, that's that,' laughed Rosie, winking at Matt. 'You're on your own.'

'Hardly!' scoffed Prudence. 'He's got most of Seabury to keep him company.'

'Here goes nothing, then,' said Matt. 'See you both on the other side.'

Rosie watched as Matt straightened his shoulders and clapped his hands to get everyone's attention –

turning from a shy boy into the successful doctor in front of her eyes.

'Come along, Rosie,' said her Nan, squeezing her arm. 'There'll be plenty of time for ogling the handsome doctor later. Let's get into that kitchen. No doubt they'll all want a cuppa when they're done... and it will take a while to find enough cups!'

Rosie felt her cheeks heat at her Nan's teasing words... but there wasn't any point denying the fact that she was having a hard time tearing her eyes away from Matt.

'I can't believe everyone came just to have a poke around,' said Rosie, supporting her Nan as they made their way inside.

'Pfft – that's not why they're here,' said Prudence. 'I mean – they *do* want to see the place, but of *course* they're all willing to help.'

'But you said—' started Rosie.

'Goodness, I'm a better actor than I thought,' chuckled Prudence. 'I only said that so that Matt would step up and take a bit of action. It's important he feels like he's *making* this happen rather than just getting swept up by things. He had enough of that after his dad died. Time for him to take control.'

'You're... diabolical!' said Rosie as they made their way into the kitchen.

'Thank you,' said Prudence, easing herself into one of the chairs at the table.

'I'm not sure I meant that as a compliment,' chuckled Rosie. 'Right… where should we start?'

'Get the kettle on,' said Prudence. 'I need a cup of tea. Then we need to hunt around for all the cups and little plates we can get our hands on.'

'Plates?' said Rosie. 'What on earth for? We've only got a couple of packets of biscuits.'

'Don't worry about that,' said Prudence. 'Kate sent some cake up from The Sardine as she couldn't come herself. Lou's got it in her bag.'

'Knock, knock?'

A quavering voice from the hallway interrupted Rosie's treasure hunt through the cupboards as she waited for the kettle to boil.

'I'll go!' she said, dashing to the door before Prudence tried to get to her feet.

Peering around the corner, she came face to face with the bride-to-be leaning heavily on her stick.

'Mrs Scott!' said Rosie.

'It's Mary, dear,' she said with a smile.

'You've just missed the start of the grand tour,' said Rosie. 'Do you want me to take you up to join the rest of them?'

Mary shook her head. 'To be honest with you, my late arrival was on purpose. I didn't fancy dealing with a crowd.'

'Come on into the kitchen!' called Prudence, who'd clearly clocked the arrival of her friend.

'Leg feeling better, then?' said Mary, raising an eyebrow as she followed Rosie into the room.

'Can't complain,' said Prudence. 'Is Lionel not with you?'

'He dropped me off,' said Mary as she took a seat opposite Prudence. 'He's off to Upper Bamton to see Arthur at the vineyard. Those two talk for England when they get together, so I thought I'd pop in and have a quick look around to see if the old place is anything like I remember.'

'Well, that's fair enough, considering you've just agreed to get married here,' said Rosie.

'We'll see,' said Mary.

Rosie raised her eyebrows. There she was, the stern, slightly scary headteacher of old. Mary Scott might have stopped teaching years ago, but Rosie still had to stop herself from raising her hand in the air every time she wanted to say something.

'I must say, it was lovely news to hear Matt's back in town – and a doctor, no less!' said Mary.

'You taught all four boys, didn't you?' said Prudence.

Mary nodded. 'Yes—before they headed off to secondary school... and then that boarding school, of course. I'll tell you this, they were all ruthlessly clever in their own ways.'

'You'd never guess it, though, would you?' chuckled Rosie as she poured boiling water into the teapot and carried it over to the table. 'I mean, they caused absolute havoc, didn't they?'

'Of course they did,' laughed Mary, rolling her eyes. 'And I seem to remember *you* joining in with that, young lady!'

Rosie grinned.

'I had to visit their parents more than once,' said Mary, 'but it was never anything too serious. They just had too much energy and too much potential to stay cooped up within the confines of this sleepy town for long. They needed to leave to fulfil their potential… it's just a shame it had to happen the way it did.'

'Poor Mr Pepper,' said Prudence, shaking her head. 'He'd be so proud of Matt becoming a doctor.'

'I wonder what became of the others,' said Mary.

Rosie turned to them with a smile. For once, she had news to share before it had reached the Seabury grapevine. It was a miracle!

'What are you looking so smug about, young lady?' demanded her Nan.

'I know what the boys have been up to,' she said, trying and failing not to sound too pleased with herself.

'Out with it!' demanded Mary.

Rosie nearly snorted with amusement at the way the two old women leaned in closer.

'Okay,' she said. 'But this is just between the three of us…'

CHAPTER 13

MATT

'That was a brilliant day… even if we didn't get a single bit of work done!' chuckled Matt as he placed the last of the used mugs next to the sink.

'That's not true,' said Rosie as she scrubbed away at the seemingly endless supply of crockery in a bowl full of soapy water. 'We got rid of those dust sheets from the ballroom. Anyway – something far more important happened today.'

'What's that?' said Matt.

'We got an excited thumbs up from the bride-to-be,' said Rosie, lining up another cup on the already-heaving draining board. 'Mary's over the moon at the thought of holding the reception here.'

Matt nodded. He'd only caught a brief glimpse of his old headmistress as she snuck out of the back door before the chattering crowd of locals could notice her presence. Even so, she'd shot him a warm smile and promised to catch up with him properly when there were fewer people around.

'Yeah, that really is good news,' said Matt, 'It'll make the hard work worthwhile. Now we just have to cross our fingers that some of the crowd will come back tomorrow to give us a hand!'

Even as he said it, his heart gave a little flip. *What if they didn't?*

'Of course they will,' said Rosie firmly. 'Has anyone ever told you that you worry too much?'

'All the time,' laughed Matt. 'It kind of goes with the professional territory, I think.'

He grabbed a tea towel and stationed himself next to Rosie, ready to start working through the mountain of cups on the draining board.

'Hey, you don't have to do that,' she said, glancing at him. 'You're probably knackered. Why don't you put your feet up while I wash this lot and get it put away? Then I'll leave you in peace.'

'Hell no!' said Matt, shaking his head. 'There's no way I'm leaving you to tidy up the mess on your own. Besides… I'm not tired.'

'Really?' said Rosie. 'Blimey – I am.'

'In that case, let me deal with this lot,' he said. 'You head home and get some rest!'

'Not a chance,' laughed Rosie, not budging an inch. 'For one thing, Nan would have my guts for garters and send me straight back. For another… I don't want to go anywhere just yet. It was nice seeing everyone today, but it's even nicer to have you all to myself again.'

Matt promptly wished he could hold onto the draining board for support without her noticing. The smile she'd just shot him seemed to have jellified his knees. It might have been a decade and a half since he'd last seen her, but Rosie Phillips hadn't lost her power over him.

Aware that she was still watching him, Matt promptly faked a huge yawn – anything to throw her off the scent!

'I *knew* you were tired!' laughed Rosie.

'Okay – you've got me,' said Matt, picking up a cup and drying it with far more attention than was strictly necessary. 'But it's nothing like that first night when I felt like I needed to pass out and sleep for a week. This is more that lovely feeling you get after being out in the fresh air all day. You know what I mean?'

'I do,' said Rosie. 'It's the best, isn't it?!'

Matt nodded. He'd forgotten it was possible to be tired after a long day – and it be a *good* feeling. He hadn't felt like this since before his dad died.

Grabbing another mug, Matt dried it in silence. Today had been an unexpectedly good day. He'd thought hearing stories about his childhood would be painful. Instead, he'd enjoyed listening to people he'd known all his life reminiscing about the antics he and his brothers had got up to when they were little.

All those memories had remained tightly sealed in a

box since Matt left Seabury. Talking about them today had been like unwrapping favourite Christmas decorations. Each memory had unlocked another, healing parts of him he hadn't even realised needed it.

'You okay?' said Rosie, peering at him as she wiped a speck of sudsy froth from her front.

'Yeah,' Matt nodded. 'I was just thinking... I feel like I owe you an apology.'

'What on earth for?' said Rosie.

'For how dreadful I was,' he said.

'What do you mean?' said Rosie, looking confused. 'Today? You've been brilliant!'

'No,' said Matt. 'I mean back when we were together—or back when we ended. After dad... you know.'

'You don't need to—' started Rosie.

'I do,' said Matt. 'I can't imagine what you must have thought of me.'

'Matt,' she said gently. 'You were sixteen. You'd just lost your dad. I get it.'

Matt swallowed. 'But I was just... awful. It took months before I even started coming to my senses. By then, I was already at boarding school, and mum had shut up the house and moved and...' He trailed off and ran his fingers through his hair. 'I'm just so sorry I didn't try to get in touch. I did think about it.'

In fact, he'd never stopped thinking about it. But the longer the silence between them stretched, the more impossible the task had become.

'Well, I owe you an apology too,' said Rosie.

'No, you don't,' said Matt instinctively.

'Hey – I'm just following your logic here,' she laughed. 'I've always been sorry I didn't reach out to you after your mum sent you to that school. To start with, I was too busy moping. I was sad about your dad, and I missed you like crazy... but honestly, the mean-girl part of me didn't want anything to do with you. I wanted to pay you back for dumping me.'

'I get it!' said Matt.

'Yeah... but after a while, all I wanted was my best friend back,' said Rosie. 'And it's like you said... I left it too long. I figured you'd moved on with your life and probably didn't even remember me.'

'How could I forget you?!' said Matt.

Rosie shrugged. 'You never came home. Not once.'

'That's another thing I should apologise for,' he sighed. 'I should never have left your Nan to deal with everything. I should have taken responsibility and done something about the place sooner. I know it belongs to the four of us, but I'm the oldest.'

'That's just daft,' said Rosie. 'Trust me, Nan's loved working here – though I think she missed having you all around. I'm not sure she ever came to terms with how your mum just shut down after losing your dad, though. Sending you all off to school like that and leaving the home you'd all shared...' Rosie trailed off, shaking her head.

Matt was having a hard time breathing around the

lump of sadness lodged in his throat. But it wasn't just sadness… it was guilt too. If he didn't say something now, he never would… and when it came to Rosie, that simply wasn't acceptable.

'You know we were talking about my brothers earlier?' he said, doing his best to keep his tone even. 'It wasn't mum's idea to send them away to school. It was mine.'

Rosie turned to him in surprise. 'What do you mean?'

'I couldn't handle staying here a second longer than I had to,' said Matt with a sigh. 'Not after finding Dad. Not after losing him. There were memories everywhere… I couldn't escape them! So I asked Mum if I could go away to school. No – I *demanded*.'

'And she agreed – just like that?!' said Rosie.

'It was something my parents discussed over the years,' said Matt. 'They always decided against it in favour of keeping the family together, but with dad gone… so was the family.'

He swallowed hard. The tears glistening at the corners of Rosie's eyes were making it ten times harder to keep his cool.

'I never, *ever*, expected her to send the others away too,' he said. 'Ewan was only eleven years old!'

Matt turned abruptly, blinking hard. Placing the cup he was holding on the kitchen table, he sucked in a deep breath as the customary wave of guilt washed over him. He'd ruined his brothers' childhoods. His selfishness had taken away their chance of growing up surrounded by the safety and beauty of Seabury House. No, it wouldn't have been the same without their dad around – but at least they'd have still had their mum there.

'It's not your fault,' said Rosie gently.

Matt could feel her standing just behind him, the warmth of her proximity soothing him.

'Boarding school was my idea,' he said. 'I don't blame them for blaming me.'

'You were just a heartbroken kid,' said Rosie.

'So were they,' said Matt, turning to face her and desperately searching her eyes for the comfort he needed. 'Anyway, that's why we drifted apart.'

'Can I ask something?' she said.

'Anything,' said Matt.

'Were you happy at that school?'

Matt cocked his head. 'Happy? I wasn't unhappy. It gave me a kind of safe space. Somewhere I could get away from everything that happened. I could focus on my studies. I had friends. Yeah… I guess I was happy.'

'Don't you think the same's probably true for the others?' she said.

Matt shrugged.

'Did you see your mum in the holidays, or…' she trailed off.

'Of course,' said Matt. 'She got a little place in Spain. Started a new life over there. Sometimes we visited her, sometimes she'd come over, and we'd all stay with our grandparents in Scotland. Never here, though.'

Rosie nodded, and Matt breathed a sigh of relief as she moved back to the sink to wash the remaining cups. He'd told her, and she was still here.

'I became a doctor for Dad,' he said quietly.

'And I'm betting he's proud,' said Rosie.

'Thanks,' said Matt. He cleared his throat. 'I just wish… I wish I'd not damaged that bond with my brothers. I wish you and I stayed friends.'

'Hey,' said Rosie, turning to him again – this time grabbing both his hands. 'We never stopped being friends.'

Matt glanced down. Rosie's hands were wet in his, and he could see soap bubbles gleaming between her fingers. She shifted slightly, lacing her fingers through his.

Matt swallowed.

Was she going to… kiss him?

Wait… was he going to kiss her?!

He wanted to. More than anything. But Matt had already left Rosie behind once. It was going to be hard enough to do it again when he had to return to real life. If he kissed her, he wasn't sure he'd have the strength to do it…

Electricity danced between them, and the moment drew taught, like a silken thread about to snap.

Matt tightened his grip on Rosie's damp hands, wanting to draw her closer…

SQUELCH!

An undignified farting sound tore through the magic as their damp palms met.

Matt sniggered, and Rosie started to giggle.

'Friends?' he said, taking a step back as the moment passed.

'Always,' she replied, grinning at him.

CHAPTER 14

ROSIE

'Uncover that potato salad for me, please, Rosie!' said Prudence, waving her hand at a giant, old-fashioned mixing bowl covered with silver foil.

'Blimey Nan, how many people do you think are going to come?!' laughed Rosie, doing as she was told, nonetheless.

'Well, we've got to keep them all well-fuelled if we expect them to work miracles on this place, don't we?' huffed Prudence, arranging line after line of finger sandwiches on a tray.

Rosie and her Nan had just spent the last hour making sure everything was laid out ready to receive the working party that was meant to be turning up at Seabury House at any moment. Matt was there to help, too... though he'd spent most of the time pacing nervously in front of the window.

'Why aren't they here yet?' he muttered, craning his neck as he tried to get a glimpse of the gates.

'Patience, boy,' said Prudence, adding another couple of sandwich plates to the pile crammed into the last tiny bit of space on the table.

'Maybe you were right after all, Nan,' said Rosie with a naughty smile. 'Maybe they really did just want to have a nose around yesterday – and now they've satisfied their curiosity – that's it, they're done!'

'Don't you start,' huffed Prudence. 'Can't you see the lad's in a bad way?'

Rosie laughed. She'd only said it to wind Matt up. She knew full well that Charlie would be along at any moment – probably with more than half the town in tow if the previous day's turnout was anything to go by.

'Ah... but he's so easy to wind up, Nan!' she giggled.

'Well, don't,' tutted Prudence. 'It's starting to work on me, too!'

Matt turned to the pair of them, glanced at Prudence, and then strode over and put his arm around her shoulders. Rosie did her best not to melt into a soppy puddle there and then.

'Thank you for doing all this,' he said, nodding at the table.

That morning, Rosie and Matt had walked down into the town again. They'd visited Ethel at The Sardine, where she'd been busy making several tins of delicious tray-bakes to keep the workers fuelled, followed by Hattie at the hotel – who'd donated several dozen pastries to add to the feast. Prudence had insisted on making enough sandwiches to feed an entire county's worth of WI members, as well as the vat of potato salad to "add a little class".

'Well, if they don't turn up, we're going to be living on potato salad and millionaire shortbread for months,' chuckled Prudence, lowering herself carefully into a chair.

'How's the hip?' said Rosie. It was easy to forget that Nan was still recovering from her fall. She was always so full of life and never complained.

'Better than yesterday,' came her customary reply.

Matt turned to her with a frown. 'You should be at home, resting.'

'Hush now, Dr Pepper,' tutted Prudence. 'You're off-duty, remember?'

'And so are you!' he countered.

Prudence waved her hand dismissively. 'Don't know when I last had this much fun,' she said. 'Gets a bit boring tottering around the cottage – even with Rosie around. No offence, dear.'

'None taken!' laughed Rosie.

'Well, if you need anything, you let me know,' said Matt.

'Don't you start fussing,' she said, shooting him an adoring look. 'I keep telling Rosie I don't need her hovering over me like a minder now that I can get about by myself again. I *certainly* don't need overnight care…' Prudence paused and wiggled her eyebrows at Rosie. 'So, if you fancy any…erm… *sleepovers* – don't hold back on my account!'

'*Nan!*' gasped Rosie, feeling a hot blush flood her cheeks. Matt, however, started to laugh.

'I missed you, Mrs Phillips!'

'It's Prudence, boy!' scolded her Nan.

'Okay – Prudence,' he said, dropping a kiss on her cheek.

Rosie grinned as her Nan turned pink with pleasure.

~

Ten minutes later, even Prudence was starting to lose faith in their plan.

'Well, I guess I'd better start putting some of this back in the fridge,' she muttered. She was just reaching for the bowl of potato salad when a rumbling chatter reached their ears.

Matt sat up from his slumped position at the table and raised his eyebrows at Rosie. She shot to her feet and ran over to the kitchen window.

'They're here!' she said with an excited squeak.

'Excellent,' breathed Matt, coming up behind her to have a look. 'Blimey!'

'What is it?' said Prudence.

'Well, let's just say I don't think you need to worry

that we set out too much food,' he laughed. 'Not if the crowd in the garden is anything to go by.'

'A crowd?' said Prudence, sounding hopeful.

'Yep,' said Matt, looking thrilled. 'At least twice as many people as yesterday.'

'Let me see!' said Prudence, standing slowly.

She shuffled over and elbowed her way between them. The three of them pressed their heads together as they peered out at the impressive working party gathering on the weedy gravel.

Gardening tools vied with vacuum cleaners. Rosie could spot at least four wheelbarrows in the mix, bearing loppers, hedge trimmers, and all sorts of other tools. Everyone seemed to be wearing either marigolds or gardening gloves, and it looked like they were all very much ready for action.

'This is awesome,' said Matt.

'Seabury has arrived,' laughed Prudence. 'You didn't think they were going to let you down, did you?'

'Even *you* thought they were going to let us down there for a moment,' chuckled Rosie, giving her Nan a little nudge.

'Cheeky girl,' she said. 'Why don't you two go out and greet them while I double-check we've got enough cups. Tell them I'll get the kettle on after they've done at least an hour's hard labour!'

Without thinking, Rosie grabbed Matt's hand as they hurried out of the kitchen and down the hallway.

'I can't believe so many people have come,' said Matt.

He didn't get any further as there was a loud hammering on the front door.

'After you!' said Rosie.

Matt grabbed the door and opened it to find Charlie on the doorstep.

'I'm so sorry we're a bit late,' he said.

'That's all right,' said Matt. 'We knew you'd turn up.'

'Liar,' said Rosie. 'This one was having kittens ten minutes ago.'

'You're such a dobber!' huffed Matt, giving her a nudge in the ribs.

'Goodness,' chuckled Charlie. 'With you two carrying on like that, I feel like we've gone back in time! You always did like winding each other up... doesn't look like much has changed?'

Rosie grinned at Charlie and then glanced up at Matt, suddenly feeling a little shy. He was still the same Matt she remembered... but at the same time, he was also the serious doctor. That was the part she was still trying to get to grips with.

'Anyway, as I was saying, sorry we're late,' said Charlie. 'We had to stop off and pick Mr Eaves up on the way.'

'Mr. Eaves?' said Rosie, glancing over at the chattering crowd. 'Isn't he the chap who keeps bees on the King's Nose?'

'That's the one,' said Charlie. He leaned in, lowering

his voice. 'He can be a bit... elusive. But he called me this morning, asking if he could come up along and help. Seems someone told him that you uncovered a piano yesterday? He was quite enthusiastic to come and give it a go.'

'What do you mean, *give it a go*?' said Matt. 'Does he play?'

'Mr. Eaves is a man of many talents,' said Charlie.

'Sounds mysterious!' said Rosie.

'Aye, you could say that,' said Charlie with a nod.

'So... what's he going to do with it?' said Matt, looking confused.

'Tune it for you,' said Charlie. 'Or at least give it a go.'

'Well... wow!' said Matt. 'I mean, that would be wonderful.'

'I thought that's what you'd say,' said Charlie.

He took a step back and gestured to a shy-looking gentleman Rosie vaguely recognised. Mr Eaves couldn't look more different to the rest of the working party if he tried. They were all togged out in a mixture of old jeans, ragged sweatshirts, boilersuits and housecoats, but Mr Eaves was wearing a smart, tweed jacket over a collarless shirt.

Rosie watched as he silently shook hands with Matt.

'Erm, lovely to meet you,' said Matt. 'Thanks for coming!'

'Pleasure's mine,' said Mr Eaves in a soft voice. He

kept his eyes downcast, clearly uncomfortable with making direct eye contact.

'Matt,' said Charlie, 'why don't you take Mr Eaves into the ballroom? Introduce him to that piano of yours and grab him a cuppa.'

'I've brought my own honey,' said Mr Eaves, holding up a jar that gleamed golden in the sunshine. 'I like a spoonful stirred in. There's plenty for everyone to try… if they'd like to, of course.'

'I'll take that through to Nan in the kitchen,' said Rosie, taking the jar from him. 'I'll be through with your cuppa in just a minute.'

'After you've done that, would you mind taking charge of the indoor team, Rosie?' said Charlie. 'And I'll set the gardeners to work!'

Rosie gave him a little salute and hurried off towards the kitchen to give her Nan the honey and an update.

∽

The jar of honey was already down to its last dregs. Mr Eaves had made the most of the endless supply of hot drinks Prudence plied him with while he worked his magic on the baby grand, and the gardeners had developed a taste for mint tea when they'd discovered that a spoonful of delicious King's Nose honey stirred in turned it into a miraculous pick-me-up when their energy started to flag.

Rosie had nabbed a sip of Matt's brew when he'd taken a break from hacking back the brambles on the south lawn... and now she had a feeling it was a flavour she'd always associate with Matt Pepper and one of the happiest days of her life.

As the day wore on, people could be found in every nook and cranny of the ground floor. The rooms bustled with life as they were cleared, cleaned, hoovered and dusted to the strange soundtrack of the piano being tuned in the background.

Rosie had to admit, she'd loved having Seabury House to herself when she stepped in for her Nan as housekeeper – but this was much, much better. With its rooms full of chattering people and a garden heaving with workers – Seabury House was coming back to life.

'If only this wasn't temporary!' she sighed, wandering outside with a pail of filthy water. She quickly tucked the thought away – right next to the one about what it would feel like to kiss Matt again. They'd come so close yesterday... but perhaps it was for the best that it hadn't happened. After all, he'd be leaving again before she knew it!

Rosie headed over towards a low bank that had been newly cleared of its thicket of brambles and emptied her bucket. She straightened up with a groan. Thank heavens they were pretty much done for the day – her muscles were beginning to feel the effects of the long hours of cleaning and scrubbing.

Popping the bucket down onto the path, Rosie sucked in a deep lungful of air. It was thick with the sharp, sweet scent of newly cut, sappy greenery. It smelled of fresh starts and new beginnings.

Wondering where Matt had got to, Rosie decided to head around the back of the house to look for him. Rounding the corner onto the South lawn, she came to an abrupt halt.

Matt was on his hands and knees, weeding the large flower bed that sat directly opposite the windows of the ballroom. It had been cleared of overhanging brambles, and the nettles had been dug up by their roots. The bed now had a neat edge, and its newly turned soil was rich and dark beneath Matt's gloved hands.

'Hi,' said Rosie, coming up behind him.

'Hey,' he said, turning to look up at her.

Rosie smirked. His hands were grubby, and he had a smear of dirt on his cheek – but it did nothing to diminish the sight of Matt Pepper balancing on one knee in front of her.

'Never thought I'd get to see you in this position!' she giggled.

Matt raised an eyebrow – then promptly tumbled sideways onto the grass as he cottoned on.

'Smooth!' chuckled Rosie.

Matt grinned at her, looking delightfully pink. 'You finished for the day?'

Rosie nodded. 'Yep – everyone's heading home.'

'Thank goodness,' said Matt, straightening his legs on the grass and leaning back on his hands. 'Not that it hasn't been brilliant – but I'm pooped!'

'Well, you'd better dig deep,' said Rosie, 'because your day's not over yet.'

'What do you mean?' said Matt.

'Nan's invited you to the cottage for supper!'

CHAPTER 15

MATT

'There, what do you think?' Emmy from *Grandad Jim's Flower Farm* stepped back to admire her handiwork. She'd driven over from Little Bamton late that morning with her van crammed to bursting point... only to be followed ten minutes later by her partner Jon – in a second full van.

Since then, the pair of them had been working their socks off, and Matt was having a hard time stopping gawking long enough to answer her.

'I can't believe how good it looks!' he said, his eyes wide as he took in the borders that led from the main gate to the door of Seabury House.

Over the past few days, Charlie's crack team of helpers had weeded and raked the gravel. The re-discovered flower beds had also been weeded, edged and dug... but that had left everything looking a bit ragged and bare.

Not anymore!

Emmy was clearly the magic touch the gardens had needed to turn the place into a venue worthy of hosting Lionel and Mary's reception. Her flower farm in Little Bamton had gone from strength to strength over the past few years, and she'd added a plant rental section to the business, offering everything from fragrant foliage to stunning blooms, all rentable in their massive pots and ornate tubs.

Using these established plants that had already been carefully coaxed into flower, Emmy had created a show worthy of Chelsea on top of the bare flower beds. She'd used everything from tall bay trees for height, bright azaleas for colour, and several bushy lavenders for their scent. She'd even dotted in pots of ivy and aubretia—their trailing, tumbling forms working wonders to soften the bare edges of the newly dug borders.

'Stunning,' said Rosie, shaking her head in wonder. She looked as thunderstruck as Matt felt, and was busy staring at the dozens of buckets planted with tulips and daffodils that brought so much life and joy to the space. 'And the display you've created in the border over on the south lawn is to die for!'

Matt nodded enthusiastically. It certainly made the view from the ballroom windows a whole lot better!

'It's not our opinion that matters though…' he said, turning to Lionel, where he stood hand-in-hand with Mary. 'What do the groom and bride-to-be think?'

'Arthur at Upper Bamton Vineyard told me you're a genius when he gave me your number,' said Lionel. 'But this is beyond anything I could have hoped for. It's exquisite.'

Mary nodded without saying a word. The tears glistening in the corners of her eyes were all Matt needed to tell him that she was happy. And right now, that was all that mattered.

'I'm so glad you like it,' said Emmy, beaming around at them all. 'It's been my pleasure – I've had so much fun!'

'Is there anything we need to do between now and the wedding?' said Rosie. 'Will they need watering or covering up or anything?'

Emmy shook her head. 'The weather's going to be fine all week, and there's no frost forecast, so they should all look after themselves. I'm dropping Mary's bouquet off on Saturday morning, so I'll nip up afterwards and give everything a water and a quick once-over.'

'I can't believe it's only two days until the wedding!' said Matt, as they all waved Emmy and Jon off.

'Speak for yourself,' chuckled Lionel. 'I've been waiting for this day for decades!'

'What I can't believe is that we got everything done with a day to spare!' laughed Rosie. 'Now we've got time for a cuppa. Fancy one, Mary?'

'No, thank you, dear,' said Mary. 'I think we just

need one last word with Charlie, and then we'll head off.'

'Where is he anyway?' said Lionel.

'Here!'

They all turned to find Charlie approaching them from the depths of the garden.

'I was just making sure the bonfire's behaving itself down there before I left it.' He joined them, beaming around at the flower beds as he stripped off his gardening gloves. 'Well, well, well, I think we're just about ready for a wedding.'

'Yes,' said Mary. 'I can hardly believe it! If only we'd been able to organise some music for the reception, that really would have been the cherry on top... but sadly, we left it a bit too late for that.'

'You never know,' said Lionel, patting her arm, 'maybe one of our guests will know how to play Chopsticks on the piano!'

Charlie chuckled as Mary raised a disapproving eyebrow. '*Not* quite what I had in mind,' she tutted. 'Ah well, we'll just have to make do with a few records instead.'

'I wish there was something I could do to help,' sighed Matt.

'Enough of that, young man!' said Mary sternly. 'You've done more than enough. I don't think I'll ever be able to thank you properly for opening up your home to us like this – and for all your hard work.'

'I can honestly say it's been my pleasure,' said Matt. 'But as for the hard work, that's definitely been a group effort. It would never have happened if it wasn't for Charlie and Rosie.'

Charlie grinned and waved the comment away, but Rosie leaned into Matt's side. He felt her warm hand rest on his back and promptly lost his train of thought.

He cleared his throat awkwardly. 'Anyway, I didn't really do anything.'

'Rubbish,' said Charlie stoutly.

'I agree,' said Lionel. 'You've been brilliant!'

'Yeah,' chuckled Rosie. 'You came back home for a rest and ended up letting half the town into your house instead!'

'Totally worth it,' said Matt, starting to feel a bit hot under the collar with all the attention.

'For what it's worth, I think everyone's really enjoyed spending time here,' said Charlie. 'It'll be lovely for them to come back for the wedding with their glad rags on!'

'Well, the last thing I want to do is close Seabury House back up again when it's all over,' said Matt.

Then he blinked… and frowned… *did he really mean that?!*

He spotted Rosie's raised eyebrows but was grateful when she didn't say anything. Matt wasn't ready to answer questions about that particular revelation just yet.

Rosie had been at his side every day, working her backside off to make sure this mad promise of his turned out well. The idea of leaving her and Seabury House behind him was getting harder and harder to bear as the days wore on. After the wedding was over, he knew he'd have to make some hard decisions.

The thought of it made him feel a bit sick.

'Right, I'd better get back down to Ethel,' said Charlie, 'otherwise I'll be in trouble for missing my tea.'

'We'll give you a lift,' said Mary. 'I want to hear how you're getting on with that speech of yours!'

∽

'And then there were two,' said Rosie after they'd waved the others off.

'For what feels like the first time in days!' said Matt, grinning at her. 'I can't believe how much everyone's done to help. Mind you, Lionel's a popular chap.'

'Yeah, that's true,' said Rosie. 'But you know they didn't do it *just* for Lionel and Mary, don't you? A lot of them remember you and your brothers. Everyone's happy to see you home, even if it is just for a little while…'

Rosie trailed off, and Matt thought he caught a hint of sadness in her eyes. He knew how she felt… but he was starting to wonder if there might be something he could do about it. For both of them.

'Well, thank you for all your help,' he said. 'I meant

what I said - there's no way I'd have managed without you.'

'It's been fun,' said Rosie.

'It *has* been fun.' Matt nodded.

There it was again. That weird *stirring* feeling in his chest. If he could enjoy life as much as he had over the past few days when he'd been tired to the point of being broken… what else was possible. He had a feeling his life could look very different if he was brave enough to make it happen.

'Do you have to rush off?' he said.

'Nope,' Rosie shook her head. 'In fact, I think Nan would be disappointed if I turned up at the cottage too early!'

Matt laughed. 'In that case, how do you fancy a quick peep at the bonfire?'

'Sure,' said Rosie.

They made their way past the point where Emmy's stunning plants petered out and the scent of freshly trimmed greenery still hung heavy in the air.

Matt wanted to reach for Rosie's hand… but he knew that wouldn't be fair. Sure, they'd been pretty touchy-feely with each other for days now, but this time, holding her hand would mean something more. It would be a promise – one that he wasn't ready to make just yet.

'Do you get the feeling we've forgotten something crucial?' said Matt, sliding onto the bench Charlie had left next to the glowing embers of the fire. It had been burning on and off for a few days now – gobbling up the raked-up leaves and piles of garden waste.

'What, you mean like bringing a cup of tea and some biscuits with us?' laughed Rosie, as she eased herself down next to him with a relieved sigh.

Matt shook his head. 'Like something else we need to do before the wedding.'

Rosie peered at him.

'What?' he said. 'You've got a funny look on your face.'

'I know what you've forgotten to do,' she said.

'What?' he said again.

Before he knew what was happening, Rosie slid along the bench so that she was pressed right up against his side... and kissed him.

'I... I can't believe I nearly forgot to do that,' Matt murmured when she eventually pulled away.

'Right?' said Rosie, blinking and looking just as dazed as he felt.

Matt shot to his feet. 'Hold that thought.'

'Where on earth are you going?' laughed Rosie.

'It's... a secret,' he said.

'What?' she laughed.

'I have to make a couple of quick calls back at the house.'

'Now?' she said, shaking her head in confusion.

'Now. Yesterday. Years ago!' he laughed, knowing he wasn't making a blind bit of sense. 'But I promise I'll be back before you know it bearing cups of tea and a blanket.'

Rosie cocked her head, and it was as much as he could do not to sit straight back down on the bench next to her and gather her up in his arms.

'Okay, deal,' she said with a little pout. 'But don't be too long… and bring cake!'

CHAPTER 16

ROSIE

Rosie couldn't believe the day of the wedding had arrived already. Just as Emmy had predicted, the weather was glorious. Blue skies stretched overhead, and there was only a hint of a light breeze coming up from the sea. It couldn't be a more perfect day for a wedding.

'Goodness, Rosie, look at the flowers!' cooed Prudence, as Rosie led her Nan slowly along the gravelled driveway towards the crowd milling around the front door of Seabury House.

Rosie had forgotten that Prudence had headed home before Emmy and Jon had finished their work on the gardens – and her delight was coming off her in waves.

'Lovely, aren't they?' said Rosie, though she didn't even spare the flowers a glance. Her eyes were busy combing the crowd for her first sight of Matt. Even after spending most of the previous day with him – grabbing coffee at New York Froth and pottering around on the beaches, Rosie couldn't wait to see him again.

Boy, was she in trouble!

It was getting harder and harder to think of him disappearing back to his life in London. Could she perhaps follow him there? Maybe build a new life for herself in the capital? A life with Matt?

Rosie shook her head. She wouldn't want to be so far from her Nan – *or* Seabury, come to that. Not now that the town had wrapped her in its cosy embrace again. Besides… Matt might not have room in his busy life for her. He'd pretty much told her that when he'd first arrived, hadn't he?

I've been too busy for a personal life.

Rosie swallowed, doing her best to will away the growing bubble of sadness.

'Goodness me, have you ever seen such whopping tulips?!' gasped Prudence, stopping to admire a deep purple beauty. 'I wonder if Matt has thought of taking some photos to send to his mum. I'm sure she'd love to see her borders looking like this after all these years.'

'Erm… I'm not sure,' said Rosie, yanking herself back to the present. Today was going to be a happy day – and she was determined to enjoy every second of it. She'd worry about the other stuff at a later date. 'I'll ask him if you'd like?'

'You do that,' said Prudence. 'In fact, why don't you toddle off and find him now?'

Prudence had a knowing look in her eye, and Rosie couldn't help but laugh - her Nan didn't miss a trick. She knew very well that Rosie's head had been firmly in the clouds ever since her evening next to the bonfire with Matt. Of course, Rosie hadn't given her all the juicy details – like the fact the pair of them had kissed the hours away under a blanket while the stars blossomed in the sky – but she had no doubt her Nan had guessed most of it.

'Go on,' said Prudence. 'Find Matt – and tell him he owes me a dance later!'

'But—' started Rosie, torn between looking after her Nan and getting her first glimpse of Matt in the suit he'd gone off to buy that morning.

'I'll be fine,' said Prudence. 'Look, here's Doris and Kathleen. They'll make sure I don't get up to any hijinks while you go find your man.'

'Shh!' hissed Rosie, widening her eyes. 'Matt's *not* my man!'

'Oh rubbish,' chuckled Prudence. 'He's been your man ever since he was a youngster. Now shoo!'

Rosie watched as her Nan joined the gaggle of chattering women and promptly joined in – no doubt filling them in on Matt and Rosie's current relationship status.

Not that there was one!

Sure, there had been kissing... a *lot* of kissing – but

that didn't mean anything… not when Matt was going to be leaving again. She still hadn't managed to winkle out of him why he'd rushed off to make those calls the night of the bonfire, but she had a sinking suspicion they had something to do with Matt taking the first steps back towards his real life. Now the day of the wedding had arrived, it felt like the moment she'd lose him again was drawing closer by the second…

Shut up, brain, we're not thinking about that anymore today!

'Hi Rosie!'

Rosie turned to find Lizzie Moore, the owner of the bike shop, smiling at her. She looked wonderful in a 50s-style polka-dot dress.

'Blimey!' said Rosie. 'I almost didn't recognise you out of your dungarees. You look gorgeous.'

'Thanks,' beamed Lizzie. 'You too.'

Rosie smoothed down the frothy layers of the soft lavender skirt she'd paired with a simple silk top. It felt strange to be all dressed up at Seabury House instead of wearing her customary pair of jeans and a jumper suitable for scrubbing floors or gardening in.

'Any sign of the happy couple yet?' said Lizzie, taking a sip from her glass of fizz.

Rosie shook her head. The bride and groom should be arriving at any minute. Only a handful of family and close friends had accompanied the happy couple to the registry office. Charlie was there as best man, and Ethel was maid of honour. Hattie and Ben had gone along too, as well as Kate, Mike, and his daughter Sarah.

Everyone else was gathered at Seabury House, awaiting their arrival. Even so, the bride and groom had insisted that their guests shouldn't have to wait for them before the fizz was popped. They'd both been adamant that they wanted to arrive to a party in full swing.

'You don't have a drink!' said Lizzie. 'I think Matt's around here somewhere with a tray full of champers.'

Rosie smiled, grateful for the excuse to leave Lizzie chatting with Mr Eaves's teenage son while she continued her search for a certain cute doctor. Coming up empty-handed after two circuits of the gardens, she decided to head inside. She was determined to discover where – and *why* - Matt was hiding.

Rosie didn't get very far.

It seemed Emmy had worked her magic inside the house that morning when she'd visited to water the plants outside. The hallway was lined with blooms, and there was a stunning flower arch over the doorway into the ballroom.

'Wow,' she breathed, making her way slowly along the hall. Lionel and Mary were going to love this!

The door to the ballroom was closed, but she hurried towards it, determined to have a quick peep inside while she was there…

'Rosie!'

The door swung open before she could reach it, and

there stood Matt, looking weirdly ruffled. He quickly closed the door behind him before she could get a look inside.

'Wow,' he said. 'You look... beautiful.'

'Thanks, you don't look half bad yourself!' she said, all thoughts of flowers disappearing from her head as she ogled him. The sight of Matthew Pepper in a suit was practically a religious experience.

'What are you up to?' said Matt, still standing in front of the closed door, almost looking like he was guarding it. He was clutching his mobile phone in one hand, and he kept glancing nervously at it.

Rosie raised an eyebrow. *What was he up to, more like?!*

'I was on the hunt for a glass of fizz,' she said. 'And for you. But I got distracted by the flowers.'

'Well, you found me!' said Matt.

His voice sounded strained, even as he casually opened his arms wide, blocking her path even more firmly.

What was he hiding?!

'Are there more flowers in the ballroom?' she said, just to see if he'd let her pass.

'Yep... but no time for that right now,' said Matt, springing into action and grabbing her hand. 'Come on, let's get you a glass of champagne and get back outside.'

'Why the hurry?' giggled Rosie as he towed her along behind him.

In answer, he held up his phone. 'I just got a text from Mike... the happy couple are due any minute!'

∼

Rosie realised her whole body was tingling with excitement as she watched Mike and Kate open the gates to Seabury House so that the wedding car could sweep in. It trundled slowly over the gravel towards the waiting guests, its cream ribbons fluttering in the breeze.

When Lionel exited the driver's seat, a cheer went up from the crowd... and when he opened the passenger door and offered his hand to his new wife, there wasn't a dry eye in the place.

A second car crunched to a halt behind them, and Charlie and Ethel emerged. Sarah appeared from the back seat, clutching hold of a flower-bedecked lead. Stanley clambered down, wagging his tail and looking thoroughly delighted at the grand welcome he clearly thought was all for him.

'Hello, everyone!' boomed Lionel, wiping a tear from the corner of his eye with a spotted handkerchief as Mary was engulfed in a round of hugs. 'Look, I don't want to make any long speeches today, especially as Charlie's my best man, and none of us know what he'll come out with later.'

Charlie grinned and waved. Ethel elbowed him in the ribs, making everyone laugh. Rosie hastily wiped her eyes on her sleeve, wishing she'd thought to bring a tissue.

'Here,' Matt nudged her, and she turned, only to find him holding his own pristine cotton hanky out to her. 'I promise it's clean,' he added with a wink.

Rosie took it and brought it to her face. It smelled of him - the scent of lemons and herbs and everything that was right in the world. Her tears promptly started to fall even faster.

'Before we get going,' Lionel continued, 'I want to thank you all for making today happen – but especially Prudence, Rosie and Matt.'

Everyone cheered, and Rosie felt Matt's arm snake around her waist, pulling her close.

'Now we just want everyone to have a nice time,' Mary piped up, 'and it looks like you've already made a good start.'

A giggle ran through the crowd as everyone lifted their glasses.

'So eat, drink, and be merry,' said Lionel, 'and Charlie will wind up that gramophone. We'll have plenty of dancing before the afternoon's done.'

'And that's my cue…' murmured Matt.

Rosie raised her eyebrows and stared up at him. 'What do you mean?'

Matt shook his head but didn't answer – he was too busy fiddling with his phone.

'What are you up to?' said Rosie.

'Wouldn't you like to know?' he said with a grin, pocketing his phone again.

'Actually,' she laughed, 'I really would!'

'Then shhh,' he said, raising one hand and gently placing a finger against her lips.

Rosie's eyes went wide, and she stared at him in surprise. She was just about to say something snarky when he shook his head.

'Listen,' he said.

Rosie went still, straining her ears... and that's when she heard it.

The soft notes of the baby grand piano drifted from the direction of the ballroom. The melody wove a magic spell as silence fell over the celebrating crowd. As one, everyone started to drift towards the house.

'Come on!' said Matt excitedly, tugging Rosie's hand so they could reach the front door before everyone else. 'I want to see the bride and groom's faces when they get to the ballroom!'

Rosie laughed as Matt tugged her inside the house, and they both raced down the hall as if they were kids again. The ballroom door stood open now, and Matt pulled her beneath the arch of flowers, not stopping until they reached the middle of the newly cleared dance floor.

There, perched behind the piano, was a man instantly recognisable... even though she hadn't seen him since he was about fifteen years old.

The man grinned over at them both, his fingers not

hesitating for a second over the complex melody they were coaxing out of the beautiful instrument before him. His hair was longer now - a mess of sandy waves - but his smile was so familiar that it took Rosie's breath away. It was a smile he shared with Matt.

'Oh my goodness!' she breathed. 'It's William – it's your brother!'

CHAPTER 17

MATT

'I still can't believe you're here,' said Matt, staring at his brother as he finished off the plate of food Prudence had presented him with from the vast buffet.

'Honestly? Neither can I!' laughed Will. 'I'm meant to be in Vienna right now.'

'Show off!' chuckled Matt.

'Hardly,' sighed Will. 'I was heading over early to grab a week's downtime before the next concert.'

'Well, I know it's selfish, but I'm glad your flight got cancelled,' said Matt.

'That's not selfish at all. I'm glad you called… and I'm glad it worked out!' said Will, staring around at the room full of happy faces.

Charlie had taken over music duties while Will took a break, and he was busy making sure the gramophone was cranking out golden oldies to keep the dancers happy.

'It's amazing to be back,' said Will. 'A bit surreal after putting it off for so long... but... it's just *right,* you know?'

'I do,' said Matt, nodding.

'So... you and Rosie Phillips, eh?' said Will, popping his plate on a table and taking a swig of apple juice. 'What's that all about, then? A quick holiday fling to get it out of your system, or...?' Will trailed off.

Matt shook his head. Rosie would *never* be a quick holiday fling, and he *never* wanted her out of his system. But he wasn't about to say that out loud– not when they were standing in a room full of Seabury's most ardent gossips. The last thing he needed was for the grapevine to start rumbling before he had the chance to sort it all out in his own mind.

'We'll see,' he said quietly.

'Speak of the devil,' said Will, raising his eyebrows and nodding over Matt's shoulder.

He turned, only to find Rosie making her way over towards them. Matt's heart did a backflip when she smiled at him.

'Hey, Rosie Posy!' said Will, stepping forwards and opening his arms.

Rosie stepped right into them for a hug and then let out a little squeal as Will lifted her right off her feet.

Matt promptly wished he was sixteen years old again so that he could rugby-tackle his brother.

Instead, he took a little sip of champagne and reminded himself to behave... this was a grown-up wedding, after all!

'Well, you've definitely grown up!' giggled Rosie as Will set her back on her feet.

'You too!' said Will, wiggling his eyebrows.

Matt did his best not to grind his teeth... but then Rosie wrapped her hands around his arm and melted into his side, and the world righted itself again. Will winked at him, and Matt couldn't help but return his brother's grin.

'So, how long are you staying for?' said Rosie, swaying slightly to the crackling wartime song drifting their way from the gramophone.

'Just tonight,' said Will. 'My replacement flight's tomorrow evening, so I've got to get back up to London first thing.'

'Flight?' said Rosie.

'Yeah – Seabury today, Vienna opera house next week!' chuckled Matt. 'Told you my little bro was a big deal these days.'

'I can totally see why,' said Rosie, 'you're amazing, Will. Shame you can't stay a bit longer, though.'

'I meant to say thanks for leaving my old bedroom as it was,' said Will. 'That was an fab surprise.'

'That was all your brother's idea!' said Rosie.

Matt shrugged. He'd thoroughly enjoyed sleeping in his childhood bedroom again. Drifting off each night under the ceiling full of stick-on stars had been just the medicine he'd needed... and he wanted his brothers to be able to have the same experience if they ever chose to come home.

'I just figured it would be better to spruce up the spare rooms instead,' said Matt. 'They'll do fine if any guests need somewhere to stay tonight.'

'Will, my man!' said Lionel, sidling up to join them. 'Are you ready to start taking requests yet?'

'For the groom?' said Will, popping his glass of juice down next to his empty plate. 'How can I say no?!'

'Wonderful... because my lovely lady wife would like a spot of Glen Miller!' said Lionel, beaming at him.

'Excuse me,' said Will, bowing to Rosie and shooting another little wink at Matt. 'I will catch up with you two later!'

'Your brother's amazing,' sighed Rosie, snuggling into Matt's side.

'And doesn't he know it!' chuckled Matt, watching as his brother sat back down at the piano with a flourish before launching into a medley of lively Glen Miller songs.

Lionel and Mary were on the dancefloor in seconds, closely followed by Mike and Kate... though they had a harder time getting in the swing of things – not because they couldn't dance, but because Stanley stationed himself right between them.

'Care to dance?' said Matt, holding his hand out to Rosie. She smiled and nodded, following him onto the floor and wrapping her arms around him without a second's hesitation.

Matt pulled Rosie in close and dropped a kiss on her hair, breathing deeply as he tried to commit the moment to memory.

'It's a shame Will can't stay longer,' she murmured.

'He'll be back, I think,' said Matt. 'He was talking about coming down for a proper visit before he starts his tour of the States.'

'America?' said Rosie, pulling back slightly to look at him. 'Wow! How about you…? Is all this talk of international adventure making you eager to head off on your next trip?'

'Not really,' said Matt. 'I'm enjoying having a break.'

'You call this last couple of weeks a break?!' chuckled Rosie as he spun her around.

'Okay, you have a point,' said Matt. 'It's been a bit nuts… but it's just what I needed to get my head on straight.'

There was something about being home again that had drained the deep levels of stress out of Matt's body. The last remnants had been burned on the bonfire as he and Rosie had kissed the night away. No, he was in no hurry to leave Seabury House.

'You know,' said Matt, 'I think I've been missing out.'

'In what way?' said Rosie, staring up at him.

'Seabury,' he said, glancing around the ballroom at all the smiling faces surrounding them. 'All these people… you… I could have had years and years full of all this fun, all this friendship…' He wanted to add *all this love*, but stopped himself. 'I don't think I've paused to take a breath since I started my medical training.'

'Surely all that hard work's been worth it, though?' said Rosie gently.

'Of course,' Matt nodded. 'I love what I do…'

'But?' she said.

'But—'

Rosie giggled and stepped back. 'Either your jacket's really pleased to see me, or your phone's vibrating.'

'Damnit,' muttered Matt, 'sorry!'

Reluctantly, he let go of Rosie and fished his mobile out of his pocket. He checked the screen.

'Sorry,' he said again. 'I've really got to take this.'

'Seriously? Right now?' she said, looking surprised.

"Fraid so,' said Matt, already moving away from her.

'But… who is it?'

'It's real life calling,' said Matt.

The flash of pure sadness in Rosie's eyes almost stopped him in his tracks – but the mobile was still vibrating in his hand… and he *had* to take this call.

Hurrying out of the ballroom, Matt snuck into the empty kitchen.

'Doctor Matthew Pepper,' he said.

'Grant Ingram,' came the curt response. 'Good to speak to you again, Doctor Pepper. Wait…'

Matt raised his eyebrows. Surely, *surely* someone of

Grant's calibre wasn't about to start singing the fizzy pop jingle at him!

'Is that Glen Miller I can hear in the background?' came the head-hunter's bemused voice.

'It is,' Matt laughed in relief. 'You've caught me at a wedding.'

'Ah – well, in that case, I'll keep things brief,' he said. 'I've got good news. That meeting you wanted me to set up - would tomorrow work for you?'

'Tomorrow?' said Matt. 'Sure, I can make it tomorrow.'

'Excellent,' said Grant. 'In that case, I will confirm things with them and email you the details. Let me just say – they're very excited – so there shouldn't be any issues.'

'Thank you!' said Matt, a bubble of excitement forming in his chest.

'Enjoy the wedding.' Grant disappeared without another word.

Matt quickly turned his phone to silent and pocketed it. Resisting the urge to fist-pump in triumph, he turned only to find Rosie staring at him from the doorway.

'Hey,' she said.

'Hi!' said Matt, beaming at her.

'Sorry… I wanted to check everything was okay… I promise I didn't mean to eavesdrop.'

'It's fine,' he said. 'So… you heard?'

Rosie nodded, her lip wobbling slightly.

'What's wrong?' he said in surprise.

'You're leaving,' she said, sounding like she was holding back a sob. 'I mean... I knew you would be at some point, but... I didn't expect it to be tomorrow!'

Matt shook his head. He moved towards her and held out his arms. Rosie instantly stepped into them, burying her face in his chest.

'I'll miss you,' she mumbled.

'You've got it all wrong,' he said with a grin. 'I do have to head to a meeting tomorrow... but not in London.'

'Oh no,' said Rosie, looking up at him in horror. 'You're... you're going back to Africa?'

Matt rolled his eyes before placing a gentle finger on her lips for the second time that afternoon.

'No. I'm staying.'

'Staying?' The word was mumbled against his finger, but there was no mistaking the hope in Rosie's eyes. 'How?'

'When I called my brother the other night, I also called a head-hunter called Grant Ingram,' said Matt. 'He's found me a role down here.'

'What?' gasped Rosie. 'You're really staying?!'

'For now,' he said. 'It's a locum position... just to give me time to work a few other things out.'

'Like what?' said Rosie.

'Like... if you'll move into Seabury House with me when you move out of your Nan's,' he said.

'Oh, she will!'

Matt grinned at Prudence as she appeared in the doorway behind Rosie.

'She will, huh?' he said, raising an eyebrow as he waited for the shock to wear off enough for Rosie to say something for herself.

'Well… I don't know,' she said at last.

'Rosie!' gasped Prudence.

'I've got a few conditions,' said Rosie, shrugging as a small smile appeared on her face.

'Anything,' said Matt.

Prudence rolled her eyes and shook her head. 'Idiot, now you've done it.'

Matt laughed. 'I mean it. Whatever you want, Rosie. I need you in my life.'

'In that case, I'd love to move in with you,' she said. 'But that dinosaur duvet has got to go.'

THE END

Falling for the Pepper brothers? Come and meet
Ewan in
A Match Made in Seabury

ALSO BY BETH RAIN

Seabury Series:

Welcome to Seabury (Seabury Book 1)

Trouble in Seabury (Seabury Book 2)

Christmas in Seabury (Seabury Book 3)

Sandwiches in Seabury (Seabury Book 4)

Secrets in Seabury (Seabury Book 5)

Surprises in Seabury (Seabury Book 6)

Dreams and Ice Creams in Seabury (Seabury Book 7)

Mistakes and Heartbreaks in Seabury (Seabury Book 8)

Laughter and Happy Ever After in Seabury (Seabury Book 9)

A Quiet Life in Seabury (Seabury Book 10)

In A Spin in Seabury (Seabury Book 11)

Living The Dream in Seabury (Seabury Book 12)

A Big Day in Seabury (Seabury Book 13)

Something Borrowed in Seabury (Seabury Book 14)

A Match Made in Seabury (Seabury Book 15)

Seabury Series Collections:

Kate's Story: Books 1 - 3

Hattie's Story: Books 4 - 6

Standalones: Books 7 - 9

Lizzie's Story: Books 10 - 12

Upper Bamton Series:

Upper Bamton: The Complete Series Collection: Books 1 - 4

Individual titles:

A New Arrival in Upper Bamton (Upper Bamton Book 1)

Rainy Days in Upper Bamton (Upper Bamton Book 2)

Hidden Treasures in Upper Bamton (Upper Bamton Book 3)

Time Flies By in Upper Bamton (Upper Bamton Book 4)

Standalone Books:

How to be Angry at Christmas

Crumbleton Series:

Coming Home to Crumbleton (Crumbleton Book 1)

Flowers Go Flying in Crumbleton (Crumbleton Book 2)

Match Point in Crumbleton (Crumbleton Book 3)

A Very Crumbleton Christmas (Crumbleton Book 4)

The Big Dip in Crumbleton (Crumbleton Book 5)

Little Bamton Series:

Little Bamton: The Complete Series Collection: Books 1 - 5

Individual titles:

Christmas Lights and Snowball Fights (Little Bamton Book 1)

Spring Flowers and April Showers (Little Bamton Book 2)

Summer Nights and Pillow Fights (Little Bamton Book 3)

Autumn Cuddles and Muddy Puddles (Little Bamton Book 4)

Christmas Flings and Wedding Rings (Little Bamton Book 5)

Crumcarey Island Series:

Crumcarey Island Series Collection: Books 1 - 5

Individual titles:

Christmas on Crumcarey (Crumcarey Island Book 1)

All Change on Crumcarey (Crumcarey Island Book 2)

Making Waves on Crumcarey (Crumcarey Island Book 3)

Fool's Gold on Crumcarey (Crumcarey Island Book 4)

A Fresh Start on Crumcarey (Crumcarey Island Book 5)

WRITING AS BEA FOX

What's a Girl To Do? The Complete Series

Individual titles:

The Holiday: What's a Girl To Do? (Book 1)

The Wedding: What's a Girl To Do? (Book 2)

The Lookalike: What's a Girl To Do? (Book 3)

The Reunion: What's a Girl To Do? (Book 4)

At Christmas: What's a Girl To Do? (Book 5)

ABOUT THE AUTHOR

Beth Rain has always wanted to be a writer and has been penning adventures for characters ever since she learned to stare into the middle-distance and daydream.

She recently moved to a windswept, Scottish island, and it is a dream come true to spend her days hanging out with Bob – her trusty laptop – scoffing crisps and chocolate while dreaming up swoony love stories for all her imaginary friends.

Beth's writing will always deliver on the happy-ever-afters, so if you need cosy… you're in safe hands!

Visit www.bethrain.com for all the bookish goodness and keep up with all Beth's news by joining her newsletter!

facebook.com/BethRainBooks
twitter.com/bethrainauthor
instagram.com/bethrainauthor